“Compelling and graceful as a novel [illegible] a deep place in the human spirit. This book avoids the pat answers and easy solutions, and instead, takes readers on a provocative, heartbreaking, suspenseful and ultimately redemptive journey through the human soul. It’s profound theology rewritten with a silken thread.”

— Marnie C. Ferree, MA, LMFT, author of *No Stones: Women Redeemed from Sexual Addiction*, and Director, Bethesda Workshops, Nashville, Tennessee

“*Letters to Jonathan* is a rare wonder, a piece that manages to be deeply moving yet free from sentimentality, wise without lecturing. Opening these letters is like peering into the heart of the human condition—sinful and sacred, dysfunctional and divine. Beavers’ prose is crisp and clean, and shimmers with a kind of emotional transparency often lacking in works from our so-called age of self-disclosure. By allowing us access into the hearts and lives of this family, Beavers reflects back to us our own duality: faith and fear, darkness and light, flesh and spirit. An honest and ultimately profound study of the complexity of relationships both human and holy, this book invites us to stare without blinking into the intimate layers of our truest selves.”

— James E. Robinson, author of *The Flower of Grass: A Novel* and *Prodigal Song: A Memoir*, Franklin, Tennessee

“Here is a great story about a dynamic man who sabotages his own success and breaks the hearts of his family and friends. Yet, in allowing his own heart to be broken open by his wise and caring uncle he finds personal redemption and a realistically restored new life. The engaging entertainment of the characters and their interesting lives feels like a porch rocker on a sunny afternoon, continually refreshed by thunderstorms of inspiring insights.”

— Dr. Paul F. Schmidt, psychologist, life coach and author of *Growing Your Love Life*, Shelbyville, Kentucky

"David Beavers has given readers a tremendous gift with his *Letters to Jonathan*. It is a book, not about one man's failure, addiction, or recovery. Rather, it is a book about us all, for we are all fragile, fractured, and in need of love and God's grace. A combination of memoir, drama, and narrative, this is a story from which we all can learn, for it is the story we all find ourselves in."

— Ronnie McBrayer, speaker, columnist, and author of *Leaving Religion, Following Jesus* and *The Jesus Tribe*, Ellijay, Georgia

"If the task of a writer, as numerous high-profile American authors insist, is to first tell the truth as they understand it, then David Beavers has done us the service of doing what a writer must first do: tell the truth, honestly facing the pain, the questions, and the quandaries of brokenness, and the path forward to a new sort of life and freedom."

— Dr. Lee C. Camp, Professor of Theology and Ethics, Lipscomb University and host of Tokens at TokensShow.com, Nashville, Tennessee

"*Letters to Jonathan* poignantly captures the human drama of success, suffering, fall, and redemption. This work recalls for me the spirit of C. S. Lewis yet is clearly original in its content and scope. Perhaps its greatest gift is finding God's saving grace in the midst of human brokenness, not in the illusive search for perfection. Spiritual nuggets of gold are to be found throughout this saga."

— Father Joseph McMahon, Spiritual Director, Associate Pastor, Christ The King Catholic Church, Nashville, Tennessee

"*Letters to Jonathan* is a powerful and well-written book dealing with fallen man before a loving God. It is insightful, compelling, challenging, heart-breaking, but most of all, as true to the realities of life as one can find in any literary medium. Through the story of Jonathan and the letters of Saul, Beavers takes us through the highs and lows of the human condition. In the end we join with the psalmist and declare, 'He restores my soul!'"

— Allen B. Kaiser, M.D., Physician and Medical Center Executive, Nashville, Tennessee

"In *Letters to Jonathan*, David Beavers has written a raw, provocative, tender story of two deeply broken men. The older shows the younger the way of brokenness and a path to redemption as both experience the healing power of unconditional love. This book is bold writing and holds nothing back in describing a life lost and ultimately found again. Don't be offended by its power or coarseness. It is undeniably real life."

— Carter Crenshaw, Senior Pastor, West End Community Church, Nashville, Tennessee

| LETTERS TO JONATHAN |

For Kathy,

Thank you for your encouragement & friendship.

David Beaver

Letters To Jonathan

THE STORY
OF A
LIFE REWRITTEN

A Novel

DAVID BEAVERS

Book design by Eveready Press

Printed in the USA

ISBN: 978-0-9837256-2-6

Eveready Press
Nashville, Tennessee

To Sally, the center of my life

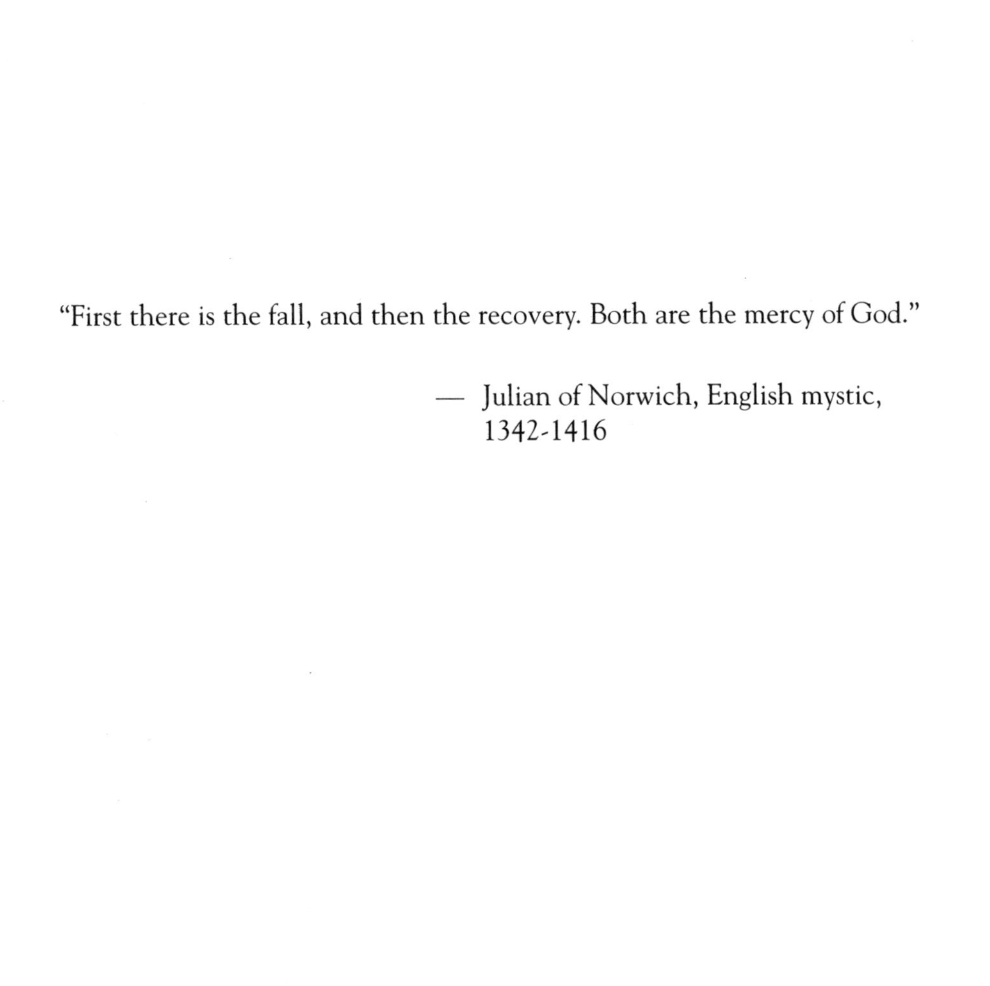

"First there is the fall, and then the recovery. Both are the mercy of God."

— Julian of Norwich, English mystic, 1342-1416

Journal Entry 1

1987

Journal Entry 1

April 17, 1987

There are days of infamy in everyone's life and today was mine – my own personal Pearl Harbor. The difference was that the Pacific Fleet had a right to be surprised when its world blew up. I should have seen it coming.

Early this morning I got a call from Barbara, a counselor I've sent several clients to, asking me to come by her office. We agreed on four o'clock, which would give me time to shower and change after my racquetball tournament at the Y. She probably wanted to ask my professional opinion about a client we both had seen.

I had a full schedule of counseling sessions before lunch. After the tournament—my partner and I crushed two twenty-something opponents—I stopped by my office and then left for Barbara's about 3:30. I parked on the street near her building, a vintage clapboard house converted into office suites, and stepped into the waiting area. There were a couple of stuffed chairs and a small table with a stack of brochures fanned out across the top. A painted bookcase against the wall held a Living

Bible and a row of books by C. S. Lewis. Still savoring the glow of victory on the racquetball court, I wondered how long this would take. My wife, Gina, and I had a dinner to get to.

Barbara came in from the hallway with a smile and a handshake. "Hi, Jonathan, thanks for coming. I'll be with you in just a minute."

I remained standing, flipping absent-mindedly through one of the Lewis books. Barbara and I had met a year ago at a seminar. We had a lot in common in our counseling approaches, and I had started sending her some of the women in my congregation who came to me for help. She reappeared in the doorway and motioned for me to follow her. The old floorboards creaked as we walked down the hall to her office, past a couple of closed doors that muffled the sounds of conversations and crying. This was a place of heartache, secrets, and life-changing surprises.

Little did I know that in fifteen seconds they would all be mine.

As I stepped into Barbara's office I caught my breath, froze in my tracks, and felt my stomach twist into a massive knot. My mouth went dry. I felt a wave of goose bumps up and down my back.

"Have a seat, Jonathan," Barbara said. Which was good advice because my knees had buckled and I was about to fall. Grabbing the arms for support, I slowly lowered myself into a wingback chair.

On the couch across from me sat two women as still as statues. One of them was a beautiful young woman I knew well. She was twenty-eight, a member of my congregation who'd been coming to me for marriage counseling. Alexa was my affair partner. The other was in her early sixties, dressed in a navy blue suit and white silk blouse. She and her family had visited my church several times. She was an attorney.

The afternoon sun filtered through the mini-blinds. A minute ago the light seemed cheerful and warm. Now it looked harsh, like the glare of a lamp over the interrogation table. I saw my car parked outside at the curb and thought about making a run for it. But where would I run? Besides, I couldn't move. I felt a drop of sweat fall from under my arm, then another.

During an eternity of silence, I looked into Alexa's grey eyes and saw the confusion and hurt that had brought us both to this moment. I looked into her attorney's eyes and saw cold steel.

We all knew why we were there. The attorney took a brown envelope out of her briefcase and pulled out the papers inside. Without emotion she read the whole affidavit, its words falling like hammer blows in the room. *Special trust violated…a line crossed…moral failure….*

I was no longer fit to serve in the ministry, the attorney continued. I was professionally and personally corrupt. I had been deceptive and manipulative, repeatedly using my position as a Christian counselor in an abusive, narcissistic way. I was subject to serious legal action that would likely bankrupt me and destroy my livelihood. My career as a pastor was over.

After she finished, the attorney instructed me to escort her to my office across town and give her all the counseling notes from my two-year relationship with Alexa. I handed them over, went back to my car and sat quietly behind the wheel for a little while. The women had done what they had to do by confronting me with my moral failure and the conclusion that I was no longer fit for ministry.

"Yes, that's all true," I told myself, "but this kind of personal crisis makes a real Christian stronger and more incisive than ever!" I was already minimizing my actions, already forming a master plan for damage control. There would be some heavy seas ahead, but I'd get through them all right. I refused to believe that forty years of dreams had been blown away in a single sunny spring afternoon.

Usually my half-hour drive home is a pain; I want to get home to Gina and the children instantly. Tonight the drive wasn't nearly long enough. The closer I got to home the tighter the knot in my stomach got. I thought by the time I pulled into the driveway it was going to wrench itself completely out and fall in the front yard.

This is our dream house, a rambling refuge from the surrounding Nashville suburbs on five quiet acres south of downtown. The shaded sidewalks are perfect for riding bikes. The swimming pool and tennis courts are a five-minute walk across the covered bridge over Sycamore Creek. It's a Norman Rockwell neighborhood we worked all our married life to reach. Gina has loved decorating our house, and is in the middle of finishing the attic above the second story as a private retreat for the kids.

I pulled into the drive and turned off the engine. As I reached for the key, I noticed my hand was trembling. What would be my first move in getting ahead of all this? At the moment I was focused mostly on the knot in my stomach and the pounding in my head. I leaned back in the seat and let out a sigh, taking a couple of deep breaths to try and relax.

As I walked through the kitchen door, twelve-year-old Blake was there with a welcome-home hug. For some reason instead of my usual squeeze back, I wrapped him in a bear hug and lifted him off the ground, holding him tight and swaying back and forth like we did when he was two. I felt hot tears brimming in my eyes then running down my face – I don't think he saw them before he squirmed free and ran outside to join his twin brother and big sister.

All around me was the safe, comfortable, predictable world Gina and I had built for ourselves and our children. How could I protect it? I had to bring my wife to a meeting with Alexa's lawyer on Monday. I had two days to figure this out.

"Jonathan!" Gina called from the back of the house.

"I'll be there in a minute." Normally I head back to see her first thing, then go upstairs to check on the remodeling. This time I wanted to go upstairs first. I needed time to think. The smell of sawdust met me in the stairwell. Stepping over a box of nails and leaning against a doorframe,

I imagined the finished space exactly like I had planned it down to the last detail. It would be, like everything else, perfect. Next week after the drywall is up it will look much more complete. Here is where Blake and Grayson's room will be; and over here is Lilly's.

As I surveyed the day's progress, my head swirled with questions. How would I survive professionally? How could I keep the kids in private school? How would Gina take the disclosure? How would we rebound when the news hit the streets?

"Jonathan!" Gina called out. "We've got to hurry. The school auction is tonight." I took another deep breath and went into our bedroom, where she was drying her hair. "How'd you do in the tournament?" she asked.

"We walloped them," I said, then went to change. Everything seemed so normal. Only I know our world is about to change forever. It's like one of those classic movies when the hero realizes a bomb is about to go off. Racing against time, he has to find the computer code to stop the fatal sequence from beginning that will lead to annihilation.

The fact is, though nobody knows it but me, the bomb has already gone off. There wasn't time to tell Gina tonight because we went to the fundraiser at Oak Park, where the children go to school. I don't know what she'll do. I'd like to think she'll stand beside me, but why should she? No, this is a zero tolerance situation. More likely she'll take the kids and go to her parents in San Antonio. My biggest fear is coming to pass—losing Gina's approval and affection. If only I can make her understand.

We got through the night somehow. I don't think she suspects anything is wrong. The spring auction was a success as always. We spent the evening chatting aimlessly with other couples—great people, hard-working Christian men and women who seem to have it all—the new cars, incredible homes, all the right connections. In the style of the Old South, acquaintances came up to chat with every pretense of friendliness, yet they were always subtly looking over my shoulder in case they spotted somebody more important to talk to.

There was the usual inane small talk:

"O m'gosh, that outfit is adorable! I love it!"

"We've got to get together soon, Jonathan. Call me next week, okay?"

"Can you believe Lilly is graduating this year? They grow up so fast!"

Several couples had come to me in the last year for counseling. I know all about the broken lives, their fears and desperate misery behind the façades of suburban upper-class success.

In a few hours, they'll know I'm one of them.

The evening went without a hitch. Donated items brought in more than $80,000 for the school, and the winning bidders got some great deals. We got back home a little after ten o'clock.

Now everybody else is in bed and the house is quiet. I told Gina I wanted to go over some notes for a few minutes. I have to figure out how to break the news to her. How do you tell your wife that your life and your marriage have been a lie? I warn counseling clients all the time about being consumed with keeping up appearances, trying to satisfy other people's expectations. That's when your heart and soul—the real you—get upstaged by a kind of image—the fake you. Now I'm facing the consequences of ignoring my own advice.

I've lived a double life for two years. Pride has been fueling my vision for a successful ministry and keeping me isolated from honest, open people. Fear has paralyzed any willingness on my part to ask for help while I was drowning in my own despair and deceit. I couldn't stand to let others see who I really am. I traded my most cherished relationships, my core values, and my intimacy with God to try and satisfy an insatiable craving to feel important, to feel powerful, to feel happy in the moment no matter what the risks.

During my fifteen years in the ministry, I've seen hundreds of people make choices that ripped their families to pieces. Now I've made some of those same destructive choices. As a pastor I've always been confident that God would keep me bulletproof. I believed this even as I struggled for all these years with lust, and with the temptation that comes from associating with attractive, emotionally vulnerable women—women who see me as a solution to their problems.

But I wasn't worried. I belonged to God! I knew that half of all married men had an affair before they were forty, and half of all marriages end in divorce. But I was different. God would protect me from all that stuff. Nothing like that was going to happen to Jonathan Goodson. No way.

I've got to try to get some rest. Tomorrow is going to be a hell of a day.

April 18, 1987

I actually slept better than I thought I would. For a minute when I first woke up I thought yesterday was some horribly realistic nightmare. The soft morning light on the window shade was dappled with the shadows of oak leaves that moved in the breeze. Then my stomach seized up like I'd taken a fist to the gut. Yesterday was no dream.

Our house comes to life every morning with me rallying the kids, fixing breakfast, and pointing them in the direction of some clean clothes. I'm usually Mr. Mom before I leave for the office, then Gina takes over. Not this day. I lay curled up on my side under the floral comforter and didn't move. I couldn't think about breakfast or anything else. Every brain cell was working on what to say to Gina. Nothing else mattered.

Gina got up and started dressing while I pulled myself around and sat on the side of the bed. We chatted quietly about what we had planned for our Saturday and what the kids were doing. The tension was killing me, but all I could do was keep up the charade. I couldn't decide if my head would explode before my stomach, or the other way around. Finally I buried my face in my hands.

"Come on, sleepyhead," Ginny teased. "Time to rise and shine."

I raised my head. "I need to talk to you about something."

My tone caught her by surprise. "What is it?"

Nothing better came to mind, so I simply blurted out the truth. Her face went completely blank, like her nervous system had been switched off. She didn't move or make a sound. All I heard was the blood pounding in my ears.

"You're kidding me."

"No."

As I told her about the meeting in Barbara's office yesterday, her disbelief changed to heartbreak. She asked questions, but didn't dig for details. We discussed going to see the attorney on Monday. Gina didn't condemn me or come down on me. She was in shock, seemed more angry at Barbara and Alexa than at me.

She sat looking out the window, the sun streaming in on her face. After a long moment she spoke.

"Well, it's nice to know that you're not God."

What did that mean? She can be sarcastic at times. Was she glad that I was a normal, flawed human being like everybody else? Was this her way of saying, "I accept your admission. I forgive you. We'll get through this"? Or did it mean something else?

The sense I got was not a warm reassurance of her love, nor was it outrage and bitterness. It was more like, "I'll get back to you on this." Looking back, I see that even though I betrayed her trust and broke her heart, we were falling into an alliance that was at the same time unsettling and comforting. I don't think love is the glue holding us together now. Rather it is survival.

The day went on, both of us pretending in front of the children that everything was normal. Gina was suffering and I was stressed to the breaking point. Getting through the day was all that mattered. We just kept going, even though we knew we desperately needed some uninterrupted time for a long, deep, thoughtful conversation.

We never had the time. I don't think we wanted it. We much

preferred letting the weekend routine keep us distracted. Now it's late. Gina told the kids she had a bad headache and would sleep in the guest room so she wouldn't keep me awake. Tomorrow I'm sure we'll continue the charade at church. Then comes Monday and our meeting with the attorney. God only knows what will happen after that.

Letters

1961-1973

Letter 1

September 12, 1961

My Dear Jonathan,

It's hard to believe a week has already passed since your mother's funeral. The last few days have been a blur. Time feels so odd. One week. Feels like an hour ago. Feels like a thousand years ago. Though Lilly was officially my sister, she was also the only mother I ever knew. How strange that I never knew my biological mother. How ironic and sad that she died giving life to me. And so it was Lilly who raised me, loved me, fed me, protected me, counseled me, mothered me. All my life.

I had hoped to see you again before the weekend. When we came by Friday morning, I was surprised that you were already back in school. Then I remembered that in high school you can't play in Friday's game unless you go to Friday's classes. Janie and I decided to stay home that evening. I hope you'll understand. Honestly, it's hard to do anything right now. I read in Saturday's paper that you ran for 74 yards. Good job! But then Pine Ridge lost it at the very end. Those are the hardest, aren't they—to have the lead for the whole game then watch everything fall apart in the last minute.

When I came by your house, I spoke to your dad for a few minutes as he was leaving. He seemed to be in a hurry, and said he needed to check on some things at the hardware store since he'd been gone all week. Gertie was there, too, doing the laundry and making beds, so I went in to say hello. She said she hadn't stopped crying since Labor Day. She said Miss Lilly was her angel from heaven and loved her more than anything in this world, and that "the good Lawd is gonna have to take care of Mista Jonathan and his daddy." What a wonderful woman.

Your dad also said that your Aunt Maureen and cousin JJ would be moving in with you on Sunday. I'm guessing that you and your dad will drive over to Canton and pick them up. How do you feel about JJ coming to live with you? He's a special kid. I've never known a more loving and tender child. Maureen has hung in there teaching and caring for him and it shows in his life. Wait until you hear him say the blessing at supper.

Your dad and Maureen are close. He's an amazing brother to her. Them coming to live with you will probably be a good thing for everybody. JJ worships you, Jonathan, even though he's five or six years older. You're so attentive when you talk to him, and good to let him join in with you and your friends. Most kids your age would be totally embarrassed—even ashamed—of a cousin with cerebral palsy. He'll finally get to see you play football. That will make him the happiest kid in the world.

I hear the Gordons invited you to stay with them for a couple of days. I feel sure Buck will be the starting quarterback at Pine Ridge next year. He's got it all, Jonathan. All he needs is some experience and seasoning. It's also a safe bet that Buck's mom talked with your dad about getting you to stay with them. It would be hard to turn her down for anything. Your dad is trying to keep things as normal as possible for you. When you figure out what normal is, please let me know.

You and I haven't had a chance to talk—just the two of us—and that's what we do best. I expect you've been wondering why nobody said anything to you about your mom when she went into the hospital. Something inside me kept pushing back any suggestion that her cancer had come back. I refused to let it in. We try to be so upbeat and positive all the time, Lilly most of all.

Damn it! She was the last one to let on that she was sick at all. Always talking about having the flu—at least that's what she said the doctors were telling her.

Jess may have known his wife was not doing well, but by not talking to you about it he kept his hope alive that she would get better again, that somehow the bad news wasn't really true. He told me three weeks ago that he wanted you to have your life and friends and play football and have a good year at school. He didn't want you to worry. Then everything happened so fast. It seems like yesterday when your mom dropped you off at school for the first day of summer practice. She drove from there straight to Dr. Rutger's office, and he sent her to the hospital the same day. Your mom had cancer but no one wanted to talk about it—including me.

I can't move, and I've already missed two days of teaching my English classes, but every one at Young Harris High School has been very understanding. Do you remember Tina Bragg, the pretty blond at Little River Church? She was in the Sunday School class your mom taught seven or eight years ago. You were probably in the first grade. She teaches a geography class first period next door to my English class, and we cross paths during lunch. She and some other teachers have been so nice to me, always asking about you and your daddy. A couple of them brought a ton of food to my house yesterday. Janie was with me when Tina came by and got very jealous. Since there weren't many of us there and I didn't feel like eating, most of it is still left. I had only a piece of chicken and a few beers.

Pastor Quinn did a good job, I think. He mentioned Thursday morning before the funeral that it was your idea to include the fourteenth chapter of John ("*...for I go to prepare a place for you. And if I go and prepare a place for you, I will come again, and receive you to* Myself*; that where I am, there you may be also....*") and to sing "How Great Thou Art." How many times do you think we've heard your mom sing that hymn at Little River Church with Pastor Quinn's wife and Liz (her last name draws a blank—the one you always called Lizard Lady because of the way her eyes dart around)? I don't think Harriet Quinn or Liz Lizard Lady have much to offer musically compared with your mother, but as a trio they sounded good. Out of respect for Lilly, I hope they won't continue the act as duet!

Did you see your Uncle Randall? Thanksgiving a year ago was the last time we saw him. They'll probably count this trip as their annual visit. As usual, he was quiet and stayed in the background, especially when he saw your grandfather walk into the church. Randall and I hugged and, as always, said we ought to see each other more often. He had been crying—his face was red and streaky—and he walked around like a zombie the whole time, though that's pretty much the way he is whenever family comes around.

You may have seen him and your Aunt Marcie more than I did. He told me they were going to spend the afternoon with your dad and drive home to Macon that night. He loves your mom so much, Jonathan. He and Lilly had a special bond that began a long time ago. But I'm told they got really close right after our mother died. It was only a few weeks later that dear old Dad, the esteemed Reverend Bates, left his church in Gainesville and started traveling and preaching all over Georgia and Alabama.

It caught me off guard when Pastor Quinn asked him to pray at the end of the funeral. Did you find that strange? I'm probably being too harsh about my father. (There, I did it. I called the sonofabitch my *father*.) He's decent to you and Randall's kids and some of the cousins—that's part of the charade as well. Your dad never says anything, but even he knows what's going on with your grandfather, especially after he got all over Maureen when JJ was born with cerebral palsy, saying this was God's judgment for her living in sin and having a baby out of wedlock. You didn't hear him confessing any of his sins when his wife died a day after giving birth to me! Wonder what God was up to back then? It's so pathetic. I'm sure Christianity suffers more from people like my father walking around "preaching the Word" than from an unwed mother working two jobs and loving her child the best way she knows how.

When I heard him giving that long prayer about how wonderful it was that Lilly was raised in a God-fearing home, I almost threw up. All his bullshit aside, your mom had an amazing heart for people—something that I've rarely seen, except that I see it in you, Jonathan. I see her tenderness and sensitivity in you, and that drive to make everyone happy and feel like they belong. I wish I had a heart like that.

We'll always look at Labor Day differently from now on, won't we? We won't remember September 4, but we will always remember that it was Labor Day. I wish it had been a more positive-sounding holiday, like Thanksgiving. "Labor Day" sounds so cold and hard. Maybe I'm thinking too much about my own mother. It's probably just some spooky superstition, but hearing the word "labor" puts me in a bad mood. That said, there probably wasn't a good day for any of this to happen.

You knew didn't you, Jonathan, when I came to practice to tell you? I saw it in your face the instant I got out of the truck. When you saw me walking across the field, you took off your helmet and just stood there watching me walk closer. I had already called and asked Coach Compton not to say anything until I arrived. But you knew. Your mother was gone.

I saw Coach Compton squeeze your arm and nod at you that it was okay for us to leave. He's a good man. One of the assistant coaches told me at the funeral that Coach Compton's voice was all shaky when he explained to the guys why you left early. He ended practice just a few minutes after we left—had them run a couple of laps and sent them home.

We didn't say a word to each other while you took off your uniform and I cut the tape off your ankles. It was such a gift to be with you like that, Jonathan, to be with someone I love—someone I care about so much, just sitting together, empty and sad. This will seem strange to you, but I'll always be grateful that I was the one asked to bring you the worst news in your life.

I don't know what's next. The path for your life seems pretty obvious. You're on track to have a great year at Pine Ridge High. When I graduated from Georgia Tech and realized that baseball was no longer in my future, I felt that staying around here, close to you and Lilly, was the right thing to do. Now my insides are all torn up and I want to put everything back the way it was—spending time with you, talking with my sister, playing baseball again. I feel so lost.

Pine Ridge must have closed down completely the day of the funeral. I've never known anyone with so many friends. Janie and I counted more than two hundred young people lined up outside the church. I hardly recognized some of the guys wearing their suits and ties. That same day, I heard that you had been elected president of your class this week. How do you squeeze so much into your life? Your dad is more proud of you than he'd ever tell you to your face.

I put seven little paperbacks on the shelf over your desk in your room. I hope you like them. This summer I've read them all plus four other books by the same author, C.S. Lewis. He's from England or Ireland I think. Most of his books are a bit deep for me, but I can't put him down. I stayed up most of Saturday night reading a book he wrote right after his wife died. I thought the time was right for me to read something like that. Let me know what you think.

Jonathan, I don't know if I feel sorrier for you or for me. You're such an amazing kid—so precious to me. I'm proud of you not just because of your grades and sports and other things, but because when I'm with you everything in my life is better. It's good to feel connected to you. Good luck this Friday in your game with Franklin County. They've got a really fast halfback but not much more. Stay low and square your shoulders when you hit the line. I'll be watching. Your mom too.

Love,

Uncle Saul

Letter 2

November 17, 1961

Dear Jonathan,

When you called last Wednesday I'd just gotten back from a teachers' conference at the University of Georgia and my brain was fried. I drove the school van both ways with six women who not only talked constantly but also at the same time. I have no idea how women communicate like that. The right side of my face was still throbbing from listening to Miss Jameson, who never took a breath in five hours. You'd think our school librarian would know the value of a period or comma! Mercy, she's big enough to have played linebacker for Tech this fall. We were the only two in the front seat yet, honest to God, her left thigh rubbed against my right leg the whole trip. And, no, Jonathan, this experience did *not* turn me on.

It was so good to hear your voice. You sounded excited about being selected to the Second Team All-State, and justifiably so. All the pictures and statistics will probably be in the paper on Sunday. I'll pick up some extra copies for you.

Except for losing the state playoffs, I'd say you had pretty much a storybook season. No one asks me anymore if I'm the Saul Bates who pitched at Georgia Tech. All they want to know is if I am related to that amazing freshman fullback Jonathan Goodson who plays for Pine Ridge. It feels like a promotion. Nobody cares or remembers about my days at Tech or how close I came to making it in professional baseball. People are like that–they only want to know what you've accomplished today. Success is such a fickle thing, Jonathan! It's here for a minute, maybe an hour, then it's gone. I'm the only one still feeding off my past glories.

I still have your letter from two years ago telling me that my shoulder was going to be okay. You've always encouraged me. Coach Wilson was letting me pitch only a couple of innings a game during the spring games we played in Florida. I was scared to death about my future and kept thinking about Kelly Stringer. Remember him? He was a senior at Tech when I came in as a freshman. No one could touch him. Scouts had been looking at him since high school. But in his last year he developed the same kind of rotator cuff injury I had. By the third game he was done.

He came down the next year for the Georgia game and spoke with the team but there was such a sadness about him. Even though he said all the right words, everything seemed empty and forced. Now he sells insurance in Chattanooga and coaches a Babe Ruth team. He's a great coach, and he married a gorgeous girl he met at church, but he'll never have the prize he once thought was within his grasp–so close he could taste it. I don't know if he'll ever get over it.

The thrill is gone for me too, Jonathan, but not for you—not yet anyway—and I'm happy about that for you. You have worked hard, you're talented, smart as hell, and you come from a great family. You deserve all the success and recognition that's come your way. I'm just hinting at the idea that a good life might be more than hearing your name over a loud speaker or seeing your picture in the newspaper. By the way, I cut out the picture of you and Buck Gordon in the *North Georgia Tribune*, "Goodson-Gordon Duo Will Carry Pine Ridge Next Season." The pressure starts early doesn't it?

You and Buck are two peas in a pod. I'm happy you can be stars on a team together–and best friends too, ever since you met in sixth grade. By the way, whatever happened to that boy you used to be such good friends with before Buck came along? He and his mom were really poor and lived in that little building behind your house that I thought was a storage shed. Mark Smalley was his name. I haven't thought of him in years. I figured he and his mother might come to the funeral, but I didn't see them.

The two of you spent every day together riding bikes, playing in your tree house. Whenever I didn't know where you were, I could find you down by the creek with Mark. You said he smelled kind of funny and his front teeth were green! But you didn't care. He was your friend and that was all that mattered. He'd sleep over on Saturday nights and go to church with you the next day. I don't think Lilly let you spend the night at his house.

Little League tryouts were hard for you then. Every year he got cut and, of course, you were chosen first. You felt so bad—I think you said *guilty*—that you stopped wearing your baseball cap when Mark came over to play. Then he just disappeared. What happens to those people who come into our lives and then for some reason seem to fade away because we move on to bigger and better things?

You've certainly moved from one success to another these past few years, and it makes your old uncle mighty proud. I get calls every week from people who know your dad asking how Jonathan is getting along now, other than football. Most of them knew your mom too at church or the high school. They want to know how you're handling things since your mother died.

I just say, "I guess he's doing all right." You seem fine. No one could be having more fun or be more popular. The question now is: what's next now that football season is over? You mentioned that you're thinking about not playing basketball, just concentrating on baseball and football. That sounds like a good idea. Give yourself a little time off to rest. It's been an incredible two months for all of us.

Except for my teaching schedule at Young Harris and coming to your games, I've had lots of time to be alone (you know I live out here in the middle of nowhere) and to think about what's next for me. Janie has become such big part of my life. We've dated for almost four years, but I haven't yet asked her to marry me. I barely make enough to support myself.

When we started dating, the only thing I saw in my future was baseball. That future didn't happen, and lately my thoughts about the future with Janie have gotten scrambled up too. A couple of weeks ago I figured it was time to return all the dishes and containers Tina Bragg left at my house after the funeral. When I did, she asked me to come in for a minute. The first thing out of her mouth was that she and her Auburn honey had broken off their engagement. That's when I should have left, but I didn't. We kept talking and before I knew it, midnight rolled around and we had finished two bottles of wine. It was real cozy.

When I got up to leave, she hugged me goodnight. Then we kissed. And kept kissing for maybe ten minutes. My head was spinning. I got home, had a couple of beers and fell asleep watching TV. The next day I felt like crap and barely made my first class.

So, I'm wondering, how does something like this happen if I'm in love with Janie?

People make life so complicated. That may be why I like seeing JJ from time to time. He looks right through the complexities and smokescreens to a person's inner core, the part that's genuine. He's oblivious to all the window dressing everybody thinks is so important, the stuff I have chased all my life. He just loves the people around him and they feel his love, boundless and unconditional. He just loves me for me. I couldn't impress him if I tried. All this hype and pressure I carry inside seem to go away when he and I are together. I'm convinced that he knows what's going on far more than people give him credit for. He'd think he had died and gone to heaven if he got to see you at the football awards banquet next month. Buck Gordon's mother called yesterday and gave me a personal invitation to attend. If it's all right with you, I might bring JJ along instead of Janie.

You seemed really upset when we talked last Thursday about your dad dating some different ladies. I was going to say that it did seem a bit too soon for him to have a girlfriend, but your concern was more about which one you liked better. I really can't believe we're even having this discussion. Where's his brain? I wasn't going to bring it up, but he did mention to me that you were angry because he had decided to stop seeing Alice Lane, the lady from Little River Church who wears the mink coat and drives the Cadillac. Nice looking, too. I also recall her saying that she has four season tickets to all of Tech's home games. Sounds like a great catch to me! Forget Janie. *I'll* marry her.

I don't know the other lady. Maureen was not impressed. She said she was tall, about five-ten, and used the word "sour" to describe her. But that's little sister talking, and no one except Lilly will ever be good enough for your dad as far as Maureen is concerned. Plus there's that territory stuff. Your mom never did like another woman "taking over" her kitchen when company came over. I could always tell when that was happening: she'd get uptight and lose her sense of humor. That's about the time your dad would become real scarce and go into the basement to be with his tools. He likes his women happy.

My best advice, even though you didn't ask for it, is to find a way to talk with your dad about everything. Help him feed the dogs after supper like you used to, and tell him how you're feeling about school or football. I remember you said you wished he would take some time to be with you and just talk about your mom and what the two of you are going to do.

He's actually easy to talk to once he slows down and feels comfortable with somebody. I happen to know that he loves you more than anything, Jonathan. He's one of these men who knows how to work hard and take care of his family, but he's not comfortable talking about personal things, especially his feelings. Probably no one talked to him when his own father died. Jess was only seventeen—this was during the Depression—and had to forget about going to college and start providing for his mother and

Maureen. All he knows is working six days a week and making sure every one is taken care of. Self-reflection was a luxury he didn't understand and couldn't afford early on, and he never got into the habit.

I'm still hurting bad over losing Lilly, but I cannot imagine what's going on with your dad. It's easier for him to just stay busy and keep moving. In the sixteen years that your parents were married, Jess and I had two really good conversations—once when we went hunting when I was nineteen, and the other day when we went over your mom's insurance. He's real gentle and kind, Jonathan, and when he relaxes and starts talking to you, he gets thoughtful. He looks up and stares out the window, like he has seen somebody he knows way off in the distance, and his eyes fill up. He's sad, I guess, and feeling those feelings seems wrong to him, like he's wasting valuable time.

Take it easy and give those stitches over your eye a chance to heal. You can't fool me. I know you think they make you look tough. Your dad said he will pick up our tickets for the Georgia Tech-Georgia freshman game. Buck and his parents will meet us there. Janie's coming and we'll all be together for Thanksgiving dinner later. It'll be great. See you soon.

Love,

L

Letter 3

December 14, 1961

Dear Nephew,

The news about your dad came as a complete shock. Twelve short weeks have passed since Lilly died—an eyeblink. To be getting married so soon is absolutely absurd. Jess seems to have been out of commission lately and we haven't talked more than a minute about anything, much less *his wedding*. He's been either working late at the store or over at his new friend's house. I guess I can see how he was attracted to her. Alice and her mink coat and Cadillac were a little over the top. But I really thought he might have better taste in women than to go for that tall, starchy number. Buck's mom told me her name is Helen Paine.

My invitation must have gotten lost in the mail. Maureen said that they will be getting married this Saturday morning in Pastor Quinn's study. Janie has been trying to calm me down about the whole thing. My outrage has been a good change of scenery after moping around for the last three months. At least I'm not sleeping late anymore. But I'm not fooled. Yes I am upset, but I know it's just anger covering up my sadness over losing Lilly. I want her back.

I can't do anything about what your dad does with his future, but when two people love each other like he and Lilly did (I prefer "do"), it seems that losing each other is every bit as important a part of their love as when they were together physically. Just because she is gone doesn't mean their relationship has ended. It has entered a very different phase, but it is a relationship which in time will give them both, especially Jess, the best way to move on.

I know that your dad still loves your mother, though what he feels now is more like intense pain. We think loving somebody is supposed to feel good all the time. But the same love that gave them so much joy and happiness is tearing him to pieces today. Maybe her, too. That's what C. S. Lewis says it felt like when his wife died. Something like, "The pain and sadness I feel now is because of the love we had then. And that's the deal."

I'm not saying Jess should never date again, but he could at least give himself a year to watch and wait as all the birthdays, holidays and anniversaries pass. The "experts" say someone like your dad should refrain from getting into an intimate relationship for at least one year for every five years you were married. That would be three or four years for your dad. And what about grieving? That's important too. He hasn't given himself the time.

I'll be all right about your dad. Just give me some time to bitch and complain. We're all going through a lot of changes. I hate the chaos, but it seems to follow me around anyway. Which reminds me that I've got my own wedding to worry about. Next April 10 Janie and I will become Mr. and Mrs. Saul David Bates, I will turn twenty-five, and you will be fifteen, all on the same day. I hope you feel honored.

Randall has agreed to be my best man, even though he thinks I'm a hypocrite for accusing Jess of rushing into marriage. He thinks that I'm doing the same thing, deciding *all of a sudden* (his words) to marry Janie. I wouldn't call four years of dating "all of a sudden." We definitely have things to work through, and we will. It'll be easier after we get the wedding behind us.

The registrar at Emory University, where I'll be getting my master's, has worked out an arrangement for me to take my first three quarters in Cambridge, England. C. S. Lewis, the author I've been reading and quoting so much lately, is a professor there and will be teaching this spring. He missed most of last year because of an illness. Normally I would not have the option to do this until my second year, but they've made an exception for me.

I'll be leaving in late January to find a place for us to live and begin classes. Janie will stay here planning the wedding and I'll come back for a week in April. (Don't give her a lot of grief when she asks you to wear a tuxedo.) We look forward to starting our married life in England. But it won't be forever. I promise to be back in the States before next season begins and get a job close enough for us to drive to your games. A perfect situation may open up for me in Chattanooga, coaching baseball and teaching English at McCallie School. It's not a sure thing, but I think I have a good chance.

As little as I've seen of your dad since Thanksgiving, I've scarcely seen you more. I know you're spending a lot of time at Buck's house these days. The two of you are together so much you're starting to look like brothers. And his mother obviously thinks the world of you. No one will ever replace Lilly, that's for sure, but it's nice to have two very different women who care so much about what's happening in your life. Seems like Mrs. Gordon has practically adopted you, at least for the weekends. She's a lot like your mom, always having kids over, cooking, and driving you everywhere. And she's very pretty, too—reminds me of a slightly younger Elizabeth Taylor. In fact, I was somewhat relieved that I brought JJ as my guest to the football banquet instead of Janie. She would have been fuming all night if she'd seen Mrs. Gordon sitting next to me in that black dress. Your mom had some great clothes, but I don't ever remember her showing up like that at a Pine Ridge event.

Speaking of JJ, he and Maureen are another reason I'm upset about your dad's marriage. What's going to happen to them? It's obvious that

Helen Paine has no use for them whatever. No one would expect them to live with your dad and his new wife indefinitely, and Maureen is savvy enough to know that. But her sense is that Helen not only wants them evicted from your house as soon as humanly possible, but also excommunicated from the family. Jess doesn't see it. And if he does, he won't react or say a word to anyone, even Maureen. Yet when he's not around, Helen quietly takes every little opportunity to let Maureen know that their days are numbered.

It's clear that JJ has never been happier than he is now living with you and Jess. Maureen's already explained to him that they will be moving very soon into their own place but he's still a little confused. I know it's a challenge for you to be with him. But his heart takes us to a different place. It's hard to describe. He needs us to take care of his physical needs, but we desperately need him to take care of us in some deeper, purer place inside ourselves. I don't know what I'm trying to say. My point is I truly believe that we need him more than he needs us.

Your dad hates any kind of confrontation, but I also know how he works. He won't drop the ball with Maureen and JJ. Regardless of what Helen may say about them, he'll take care of his sister and her boy. He might do it behind the scenes, but he'll get it done. I wouldn't be surprised if he already has a place for them rented and furnished near the store on Howell Mill Road.

Maureen won't be bitter about leaving. She's a better person than I am. Her faith in God holds her together and keeps her moving forward. JJ was born in 1941, four years before your mother and daddy got married. JJ's father was named Frankie. I don't remember his last name. He shipped out to Pearl Harbor before he knew Maureen was pregnant, and when he came back he was real messed up. JJ was three years old. He couldn't accept how JJ was and started abusing both of them, hitting them a lot. Maureen and JJ moved in with the preacher and his wife at the Methodist church in Pine Ridge. They stayed two years until Maureen got on her feet. Frankie joined the Merchant Marines and no one has seen or heard from him since. He's probably dead.

JJ will be twenty years old next month. He's never missed a meal and always had a place to sleep and plenty of clothes to wear. Loves every soul he's ever met. He tells me the most important thing is that his momma and Jesus love him. He can't read, but he knows parts of the Bible like they were written inside of him. When I think about the way JJ has been loved and cared for, it's easier for me to believe things will probably work out for me too. It only takes about two hours, though, for me to lose that sense of peace, and I'm back living the only way I know how.

Fill me in on your dad's wedding this weekend and I'll see you Christmas Eve to open presents. Why don't you and Buck plan to spend New Year's Day with Janie and me? We'll watch all the games. You can let me know when I see you.

All the best,

S

Letter 4

April 20, 1962

Dear Jonathan,

Greetings from Magdalene College, Cambridge. I've been here almost a week and this is the first minute I've had to catch my breath and write you a proper letter. Janie and I are settled in our bed-sitter, which is a veddy British (and decidedly more romantic) term for an efficiency apartment, a block from the college. Janie seems to love the place. Especially the fact that it comes with a servant who wakes us with a knock on the door every morning, makes the bed and tidies up while we're at breakfast, and does little chores and errands for us and the other couples on our hall.

Of course Professor Lewis is absolutely mesmerizing. He is the perfect Cambridge don, dressed in bulky tweeds, black-rimmed glasses, usually with a pipe in his hand. It's easy to forget his Christian pursuits are entirely on his own time. Officially he's professor of medieval and Renaissance English. Perhaps the best thing about him as a teacher, other than his friendliness and accessibility, is that he doesn't deliver any pat answer to anything. He has this uncanny ability to frame solutions in such a way that you almost can't avoid reaching them, yet you somehow think you got there on your own. It's going to be a fantastic summer.

Before we flew over, we had a two-day honeymoon in Atlanta. Randall did a good job driving us over in Janie's car, losing everyone who gave chase from the reception. When we got to Mt. Paran Road we pulled in the Swensons' driveway and waited for everybody to go past. I haven't seen Randall as animated or happy about anything as he was at our wedding.

Rather than just dropping us off at the hotel, he actually got out and helped carry our luggage to the front desk. While we stood there waiting for the room key, he presented Janie and me a chilled bottle of champagne and two glasses like they were awards of some kind. Then he wrapped his arms around us in a tight little huddle and said, "I love you, little brother. I love you, Janie. Have fun." He was crying a little. His other self, the infamous zombie brother, was nowhere to be seen. He seemed so different, so content. He was a little hyper from all the excitement, but so gracious and attentive. He never drinks, so I have no explanation for his behavior. He even volunteered to wash the car and park it at Maureen's. Janie and I just stood there stunned and grateful.

In case I forgot to tell you, Happy Birthday! If we had waited another year, you could have driven the get-away car. The day I turned sixteen I "borrowed" Lilly's car and proceeded to get two tickets, one for speeding and one for speeding the wrong way on a one-way street, thirty minutes apart, though I was absolutely sober. I must say I was nothing of the kind (sober, that is) at the reception. Janie has forgiven me—I hope—for getting a little sloshed. I didn't drink all that much, it's just that I hadn't eaten a thing all day.

If Lilly had been here, I know for a fact that the reception as well as the wedding would have been at Little River Church which, of course, would have taken every ounce of alcohol out of the equation—and eliminated about ten of my fraternity brothers. They would have gone straight to Perkins Market the minute the ceremony ended, bought a trunk load of beer, and then disappeared for the rest of the night. They love me and Janie as much as a bunch of jocks know how, but some things trump even the best of friendships and free food. As it turned out, they went by Perkins *before* the wedding (big mistake), skipped the wedding and went straight to the country club.

You helped create a special memory for Janie and me at our wedding. Janie almost broke down while you were reading I Corinthians 13: "Love is patient, love is kind, and is not jealous...love bears all things, believes all things, hopes all things, endures all things...." You seemed to be very relaxed even with all the people watching you. By the way, you looked extremely elegant and grown-up in your tux; thanks for wearing it.

The whole scene—except for the tux, of course—reminded me of when you gave the sermon on Youth Sunday last summer, just before your mother went into the hospital. I'll never win a perfect attendance pin at church (my father cured me of that) but Lilly's insistence persuaded me to come to hear my nephew preach. I was absolutely in awe. You're a natural.

The church was packed and, as the cliché goes, we could have heard a pin drop. I can't recall a thing that you said (sorry), but you came across confident and well prepared. It was as if you were just talking with us, not at all *preachery*. It was hard to believe it was a fourteen-year-old kid up there in the pulpit. It felt more like a satisfying conversation with an old friend. Of course I'm prejudiced. What can I say? You're my hero in so many ways. I can't be objective at all. But still, you did a great job, both last year and at the wedding.

With all the matrimonial commotion and my leaving for England, we'll have to celebrate our birthdays together later. Maybe we'll do it when Janie and I return in late August. I can't think of a birthday without thinking of you and Lilly. You and I have had every birthday together since you were born. The biggest bash ever was the surprise party when I turned fourteen. You were just four, but you were there because she and your dad pulled the whole thing together at your house. When I came over that night, I thought we were just going to grill some burgers and have cake and ice cream. Lilly asked me to get the ironing board for her. It always hung behind the door going down to the basement. I took a few steps into that dark little hallway where you had to reach out for the string hanging from the ceiling, and before I could find it: BOOM! The lights came on and all of my friends appeared out of nowhere, kind of the reverse of how cockroaches scatter when the light comes on. They scurried out of cracks in the wall, through windows and doors, from behind drapes and furniture. Lilly invited every person who meant something to me and every one of them came. My heart was in my throat for two solid hours.

I still think about that party all the time. What sticks most in my mind was how loved and accepted I felt by everyone. Lilly sure knew how to make me feel special. I was practically living with the three of you anyway. Randall was married, so it was just me at home. And there was no way I was going to hang around when dear old dad, the distinguished Reverend Bates, was in the house. Fortunately he traveled Wednesday through Sundays, preaching. Thank God, my birthday was on the weekend that year. His absence made the occasion even more perfect.

My friends and I listened to records and played pool all night. Except for Valerie Gamble, the girls stood on one side of the room and the boys on the other. Valerie had been my girlfriend since the fourth grade. Actually she was more of a best friend; I never stopped liking her. I remember I cried for two days when she moved away. The last time I heard from her was the day before her wedding. She was crying when she called. I could tell she was really afraid about everything and just wanted to talk. Janie and I were serious at the time, but not engaged. I felt really strange because it was so easy talking with Valerie—like we'd never lost touch. We talked about why we never got together and by the time we hung up, there was just this deep sense of gratitude that we had been a part of each other's lives. Absolutely no regrets. When we finished talking she seemed fine. I think about her from time to time, usually when I'm feeling lonely. I don't know why.

And so, the party tradition continues—a beautiful wedding and another great celebration. Buck Gordon's parents were very generous in arranging for the reception at their club. The last time I went to Iroquois was eight years ago, when a cheerleader from North Cobb and I parked one night next to the tennis courts. Not exactly a party, but a very memorable time.

Technically then, the wedding reception was the first time for me to actually be inside the club. Janie enjoyed every minute being the center of attention and receiving all the love. I don't know how she pulled it off. While I was in school she worked two jobs to pay for most of the wedding, and we used some of Lilly's insurance money to pay for the club.

I must say, Buck's mom clearly has a thing for her son's football buddies, especially Pine Ridge's star player, Jonathan Goodson. I would not have been as passive as Mr. Gordon about my wife's flirting with all the young studs. She kept saying, "Mrs. Gordon is my mother-in-law! Call me Teri!" Her husband appeared good-humored about her party spirit. I saw him sitting with your dad and Helen Paine, apparently unaffected, chatting quietly and nursing a drink throughout the evening. I can't get a read on the man.

I had a couple of hours to spare Friday before the rehearsal, so I went to see Maureen and JJ. She met me at the Atlanta Humane Society where she's working. She loves animals, so this is a good fit. Their duplex is exactly halfway between the Humane Society and your dad's hardware store three or four blocks over. We walked down to check on JJ and he was excited to see me. Of course he started talking about you the minute we walked in the door and never took a breath. Gertie's sister Minnie stays with JJ during the day and works for your dad at the store in the evenings. Maureen feels good about his situation, and your dad is able to come by and check on her and JJ without Helen's knowing.

Maureen and JJ both came to the wedding, but Maureen told me she didn't feel comfortable coming to the reception. She knows Helen doesn't like her and that your dad feels caught in the middle. No doubt Helen would make it difficult if she saw Maureen and your dad talking together:

she figures they're talking about her. I hope you understand that the way Helen treats Maureen and you and your friends has nothing to do with anything you have done. Every person she meets she sizes up as a threat or a stepping-stone to her feeling special. She has a huge need to be not only the much-loved and worshiped wife of Jess Goodson, but also the only person loved and worshiped by Jess Goodson.

Helen is truly high-maintenance, not to mention a "pain" in the ass—no pun intended. People like her are bottomless pits. They never have enough. They're full of contempt and nothing we do for them is ever good enough. That's how they control us, by letting us know that we don't quite measure up. We live in the mysterious land of "not-enough-ness."

Maureen says Helen has been working on you lately, planting crazy ideas about how your dad is unhappy or upset with you. I know how much you want to please your dad, which makes it extra hard since he doesn't really talk about much with you. You have to sort of read his mind. Don't let her contempt and manipulation drive a wedge between you and your father.

Don't let her undermine your confidence either. You and I are alike in that regard, Jonathan. We want people to like us and when they don't, we feel guilty. We think, "Have I done something wrong?" And even though I know all this crap, I still keep trying to please these people. Like Reverend Bates. As mean and harsh as he is, something in me longs for his approval. I honestly don't think he has it to give, or Helen either for that matter. So why do we keep trying?

It will be so strange being in England during baseball season. While you're slugging it out on the diamond, I will be suffering withdrawal in a land where baseball is practically unknown. I don't think I'm a likely convert to soccer, or to rugby or cricket either for that matter. Good old American sports are in my blood to stay.

Please keep me up to date on your games.

Cheerio,

S

Letter 5

September 8, 1962

Dear Jonathan,

You made a good observation last week at the family picnic—the remark about our pace of life and whether or not, after a certain point when growing up, we must start running frantically and not stop until we are very old and dying—or dead. An appropriate thought for Labor Day. Life certainly feels that way to me. Today is the first chance I have stolen to collect my thoughts, slow down and listen to my own heart. Janie and I are both exhausted and frazzled. I am missing Cambridge and my special connections there. More about that later. Right now, Janie and I are desperately trying to figure out how to keep our sanity. She has gone back to work and my classes at Emory never seem to let up.

I use the term "family picnic" rather loosely. "Family zoo" is probably a better description. I'm glad someone chose Chastain Park for this unique occasion. Most of the family knows that it's legendary for all the dark and hidden places where couples make out, especially the Witch's Cave. I have no idea how you got away with your sarcastic comment, something like, "Well, Helen, how does it feel to be returning to your place of birth?"

She either didn't hear you or just chose to ignore the remark. Those who did hear you thought it was hilarious (thus the snickering) and long overdue.

Please tell me something. How in the hell did my old man get invited to this thing? I'm sure the distinguished Reverend Bates was pleased to have on hand one of his favorite sermon illustrations, Maureen and JJ. In the future, try to remember that any event involving our family must always be in the outdoors just like this picnic. Never at someone's house, not even a high school gym. In other words, our family should avoid meeting in enclosed spaces. Some of us would never come out alive.

Yes, you're right that I was upset when we were driving home. Nothing—not a word—was said to me or Janie or anyone about the fact that it's been exactly one year since your mother died. Not even you. And when I did say something about missing Lilly so much, everyone got quiet. People dropped their heads (in shame?) and shuffled away to get food or refill their drinks. Are we so completely obsessed with Friday's game or who brought the fried chicken that there's not a second for us to comment on what happened last year on that Very Hard Day?

The most conspicuous thing at this picnic was your mother's absence. But it never came up. The more we danced around The Fact, the more fidgety we were acting, the more superficial our conversations became. Let's see, what did we talk about? Surely there's something that would help us all feel safe and walled off from each other, or help us avoid appearing sad or depressed (heaven forbid!). Well, there's always your football season and how incredible you and Buck are playing this year. Just as the sports writers predicted, the Pine Ridge Raiders are now 3-and-0, thanks largely to you two.

There's also the topic of your dad: the fact that he's working 80-100 hours a week, hasn't been hunting once since getting married to Helen, and plans to open three new hardware stores next spring. And by all means, let's encourage Helen to tell us for the third time how well the redecorating of your home is progressing. What's the style? I think it's called Early Brothel. Or best of all, we can ask (no need to beg) Mr. Bates to recount all of "the great things God has been doing" and how many souls were saved last Sunday night in Huntsville as the result of his "anointed" preaching. Pardon me while I gag.

I do stand corrected, however. Not everyone in our family is ignoring the anniversary of your mother's death. I went by Maureen's last week and spent some time with JJ. He quoted to me the Twenty-third Psalm, a sure sign of Maureen's investment of love and time. He also reported to me that he has not seen you for a long while. He wasn't upset, he just misses you. There were some tears, and Maureen said a prayer for everyone, even Helen the Paine and your dad. She's good at that stuff.

I was sad to learn that Gertie no longer works at your house. After thirteen years of tireless labor and absolute devotion to your parents, she was, according to Helen, "too close to Jonathan's mother to be a loyal employee." In other words, she got fired and your dad said nothing about it, except the next day he put her on his payroll without telling Helen. So, sweet Gertie now takes a city bus to the store every morning, spends twenty minutes making the coffee, then walks up to JJ's before Maureen goes to work. For obvious reasons, please don't tell anyone about this arrangement.

Janie and I have run ourselves to exhaustion. We piled way too much on our plate this first year of our marriage. Money-wise we did okay, but the pressure of setting up house in Cambridge, going to classes and all the new surroundings got to be overwhelming. We were disappointed that we didn't get to travel as much as we had hoped. There just was no time to spare. My favorite professor, of course—the reason I went there in the first place—was C.S. Lewis. He actually lives in Oxford, where he taught for decades, and takes a train to Cambridge on Monday for the three days of classes, then rides back home on Thursday. His classes (I got to take two) were extremely demanding, but worthwhile. The best experiences at Cambridge, though, were the informal gatherings and discussions outside the classrooms, in a professor's quarters or at a pub around the corner.

You may remember the book I was reading last fall after Lilly died, *A Grief Observed*, the one Professor Lewis wrote only a month after his wife died in the summer of 1960. The man is so honest, Jonathan, about his own personal and emotional life, especially about the death of his wife. Even so, his openness in person was something totally unexpected. He's such a brilliant author and teacher I figured he'd be some kind of intellectual snob or egghead, but he was just the opposite. He and I had really good conversations on two occasions. The first time we talked about my father and his strange religious beliefs, and all the stuff that's had me confused for so long. The second time he had me going on for a couple of hours about Lilly and you and me, and how her sickness and death affected all of us. He seemed to understand why I'm still unhappy and unsure about my future. I'm glad we spoke, but it was very difficult for me.

I'm still sorting out this whole idea of revealing our feelings, which requires admitting you don't have all the answers and that you're not nearly as buttoned up as you want the world to think you are. I know Jess loved your mother, but I would faint to hear him talking about Lilly the way Lewis spoke about his wife. I have never—not once—heard my father calmly talk with me or anyone else about any of his fears and doubts. I have seen him beat the shit out of Randall in a fit of rage; that is not what I mean by learning how to express anger or sadness. I can't imagine Mr. Bates ever admitting he was wrong.

Anyway, Professor Lewis strongly recommended that I start writing my thoughts and feelings in a journal or notebook. So I've started, and so far I think it's a good idea. So much of what I experienced with Lewis felt like the opposite of how things ought to be. It makes me feel weak and embarrassed to admit a mistake or to confess how sad I feel about something personal, like missing Lilly so much. I'm convinced that people will think less of me. But when Professor Lewis talked about his own doubts and struggles, I respected him even more.

On a somewhat related note, I appreciate your concern but you were a little off base when you questioned how happy Janie and I are right now. The question implies a mistaken assumption on your part. You never saw your mom and dad fight, so when you see Janie and me arguing, it's only natural that you would worry about us. The fact is we're doing great. I love being married and I recommend marriage to everyone if you find the right person. And I believe I have.

Not that it's all heaven on earth—no relationship is. Sometimes she acts like all the thinking and reading I do keeps me from really being as happy as she thinks I should be. I don't think it's realistic to expect constant happiness and bliss in any marriage, especially the first year. That's the fairy tale thing most women buy into when they get engaged. A disagreement or forgetting an anniversary makes a woman feel like the world is coming to an end. I don't buy that and neither will you. When I drink with a buddy or while I'm studying, that's something she must learn to deal with. I'm hoping she'll see that her fears that connect me to her dad's reckless drinking are irrational and, quite frankly, offensive and judgmental. At some point, she's going to have to understand that my having a glass of wine is not the end of the world. Besides, I always have Mr. Bates to remind me how worthless and sinful I am. I don't need you or Janie to keep me straight.

That sounds a little harsh and I don't mean it to be. It's just that I want to be as clear as I can with you and with Janie about who I am and how I believe life should be lived. I've always tried to be honest with you, Jonathan, and as we both enter new stages of our lives, the nature of that honesty transforms along with us. I don't know exactly what I'm trying to say. What I do know is that I love you and value our friendship. I know you value it too, and for that I'm grateful every day.

Yours faithfully,

Saul

Letter 6

January 18, 1963

Dear Jonathan,

I do find it strange that you and Jess have been to the cemetery only once since Lilly's funeral. I wonder if that's a symptom of what's going on inside, a way to cope with missing your mother. When she was here, she literally held everything together, as proven by the fact that now that she's gone, everything is going to hell. I don't think it's because she is dead, but rather because we refuse to talk with each other about her. We refuse to let her be with us in this new and difficult way. *We miss her*—three words we cannot say because they make her absence real, and that's something we can't bear.

It's easier when I'm with Maureen and JJ, but I still end up crying. The hard part is that we know what has to happen for any kind of sanity to return to our family. We have to embrace it all: her amazing personality and love when she was with us, and her abrupt and rude exit from our lives. The deep richness of the memories and also the tearing away.

I think I have visited her grave almost every week except when we were in Cambridge. Am I praying for her? I don't think so. Maybe for me and you. Maureen will know more about the value of praying. Lewis, I believe, is greatly misunderstood about the idea of "praying for the dead," which is one of numerous reasons why Mr. Bates is sure Lewis is going to hell. I think when people pray, they are in fact always praying for the dead, either those in the grave or those on the way. That just about covers all of us. Doesn't the Bible say something about all of us being dead?

Over the months since I've been going to the cemetery, the contrast in the weather and in the mood there have been striking. A year ago it snowed two inches. It was perfect, like everyone sleeping there must be more peaceful all snuggled in together, sharing this one big fluffy white blanket. On sunny days, it's quite nice in a different way. Last summer I finished a five-mile run in 96-degree heat, then stretched out on the grass next to your mother's grave.

Whenever I'm there, whatever the season, I could care less about the weather. I have no idea how long I stay. The best guess is four or five cigarettes. And I always go alone. Janie went with me the week before our wedding and departure for England. A kind of bon voyage, giving Lilly a chance to wish us well. But Janie hasn't been back since. Sometimes I just sit and stare and other times I think we're having a conversation. We talk mostly about what happened when I was a little boy and how she, Randall, and I survived childhood with Mr. Bates.

How can any of us ever grasp what happens to a family when someone we love as much as we loved Lilly leaves us? My own mother left us when I was born, but I've never been quite sure what I should be missing, other than what others my own age actually had—which was a mother. I would love for you to tell me what having a mother is like, but I'm not sure if you will ever offer that gift to me now. Our relationship is changing so much, along with everything else in our family.

Though so much has changed, here's the deal: *things* don't change, *we* change and the way we connect to each other changes. She was always there in the background, our safety net, listening to us, speaking with us, encouraging us, giving us a reason to get along and to love each other. No matter what its problems, a family is more than the sum of the individual members. When someone is missing, that mysterious sum which defines the family changes value—changes its shape, color, texture. Lilly's presence altered our moods. It makes sense, then, that her absence would create an entirely different mood.

We knew how it felt to be loved, because we were. Our home was safe and warm like a cocoon. Safe is a good word—safe, loved, and protected. If these are the moods she brought us, that must be why we feel less safe, even with each other, less protected. The atmosphere is more chilly now, like the cold winds at the cemetery. And, yes, painfully hollow. Life will never be the same.

Changes in life are both inevitable and very necessary. While some are painful, others are essential and good. Growing older is inevitable. But what about growing up? Judging from the people in our family, *that* appears to be optional.

Growing another year older will certainly change your life in a few months. You'll be sixteen! The Great Day will have come at last, The Day every young American boy anticipates! Not his baptism or bar mitzvah or promotion to Eagle Scout. It is The Day of the Driver's License. The Day of Independence. Freedom. Sex. Girls. Drinking. Acceptance. Popularity. This is how we in America transition our young boys into adulthood. I think we are insane.

Like everything else in your life, this transition has been affected by the loss of your mother. I must admit I see something in your attitude that troubles me deeply. I hope you won't be too upset with what I am going to say—God knows my life is hardly an example of how to live.

Before I say it, however, I must apologize to you again (I think this is the third time) for what happened three weeks ago at Christmas. Especially after you stuck your neck out and insisted that Janie and I get invited to your home, which meant overriding Helen and risking her wrath.

I'm sure Helen felt totally vindicated after we arrived an hour late and drunk out of our minds—not unusual for me (unfortunately) but a rare occurrence for Janie, who blamed me for the whole scene. I denied it at the time, of course, but I'm sorry to say that each passing day my memory of that night recovers a little more, reminding me what a complete fool I really was. The next day Janie was not only sick as a dog, but also humiliated beyond belief. She knows she should call your dad or Helen and make some kind of overture or apology, but she's too embarrassed. She doesn't know what to say. Jess tells me it's all right now, it's over and done with, but that Helen is still stewing.

Now back to your attitude about your mother. The day we buried Lilly we buried our heads in the sand, pledging to each other, *Nothing has changed. Lilly is dead. Act normal.* Yes, life does go on. But until we acknowledge the loss, unless we embrace the huge hole that she left in our lives, we will keep running from each other, pretending to be something we're not. That pretending and phoniness and denial spill over into everything else. It becomes the norm, defines the way we are with each other.

I can't live that way, Jonathan. I refuse to. My problem is that I'm hung up on the way you and Jess and everyone else have buried your heads and your hearts. I'm mad at Lilly for leaving us. I'm pissed at you and Jess and the others for acting like it didn't happen. I hate Janie for telling me to get over it.

Why am I so upset with you, Jonathan? That's a good question. Maybe it's because I think I don't know you any more. It feels like you've left me. Was Lilly the only glue that held us together? Probably. Even from the grave she remains the emotional core that made *us* who *we* were. She could look at our confusion and understand that it was just the backside of a beautiful tapestry others couldn't see.

I want to shake you, tell you to WAKE UP! You're not the same person you were. It's not the two inches taller you've grown or the twenty pounds of speed and muscle you've added to your body. It's your heart—the Jonathan that no longer has time for me and your dad and Maureen and JJ.

What's happening? What are you doing? I am guessing it's only the normal Asshole Period when every 15-year-old turns into a frightening creature. It reminds me of the movie we used to watch on the Late Show after the adults were in bed, curled up under a blanket on the den couch. Lon Chaney, the original Werewolf, was teamed up with Bela Lugosi, the original Dracula. You must remember the scene. Chaney stands in the light of the full moon and watches hair cover his entire body, while his nails lengthen into claws and his teeth morph into flesh-ripping fangs.

This may be the best explanation I can accept of what's happened to you. My hope is that when you're older the hair and teeth and howling will go away. But in every feature, it took a wooden stake or a silver bullet through the heart to kill the monster in order for us to see one final time the man (or boy) as we once knew him.

I'm not sure exactly how to apply this remedy in your case, but the whole matter is so frustrating and troubling to me. Are you drifting because you're almost sixteen and completely wrapped up in yourself and your harem of cheerleaders and football? I've never seen such a sad transformation in a person's life, to go from being so involved and a part of everything to becoming this self-centered child who thinks only of himself and takes everything so damn personally.

You've become so touchy. There's nothing we can talk about and feel open and safe with each other. I feel your distance and patronizing attitude. You're such a loner now when it comes to family, but quite the life of the party when it comes to spending time at Buck's house. Jonathan, I know about these things. I've been down the road you're on now. Sports, the fame and the glamour, the audience, the fans, the team, winning—that's all there is it seems. But these are dark holes where kids and adults lose themselves because their own lives are fragmented and detached from their hearts. I threw myself into baseball because I loved playing and I loved my teammates. The Game also took me away from the hell of my dad's abuse and control.

I both found myself and lost myself in baseball. The Game was my escape, yet it didn't solve any problems. It only covered them up and gave me a little break. I shouldn't be surprised that you're trying so hard to ignore your feelings, or that your dad is doing the same. Jess is stuffing his anger and sorrow deeper and deeper inside where it will do nothing but fester. It's the kind of sadness that won't go away until it's embraced and acknowledged as the right thing to feel for a season. It's the sadness of losing the love of his life. Right or wrong, Lilly was and is his life, and that emptiness and sadness drive him further away from you and from life in the present, not to mention from his new wife. The house Lilly filled with such grace and beauty is now expensively redecorated but cold and barren. Really ghastly.

You're not as naïve as I've been describing. You know what's going on. In a flash of transparency and honesty, you showed me that you know your father is miserably unhappy. You didn't want to talk about it any further. Still, you felt it. You've seen it. What could be more disheartening, even frightening, for a teenage son than to find his father hunched over the kitchen table in the middle of the night, quietly sobbing, with a picture of his dead wife in his hand? And when he looks up at you, all he can say is "Are you hungry?" The answer is yes, we are desperately hungry for something. I just don't know what it is. Neither do you. Neither does Jess.

Why three in the morning? It's the only time he can let down without feeling scrutinized by Helen. She should be his helpmate, his strongest supporter and confidant. Instead, she's part of the problem. Helen is one whacked-out woman, erratic and disturbing from the start. I wonder if your father knew before they were married that she had a grown son in California. There's no telling what other secrets may be lurking out there. She's no help to Jess whatever at this point. He has to grieve in the middle of the night because that's when neither she nor anyone else can see him weak and hopeless.

It must be a terrible time for him. During the day he's busy and distracted. But in the small hours after midnight he has no cover. The chatter of the day dies down and all he can hear is the weeping in his soul. The grieving that's actually good and necessary and normal rushes at him along with the shame and embarrassment that come from being human. All of that floods his life. Strangely, it feels like failure.

He hurts so much! Don't you hurt, Jonathan? Don't you want just one more day to tell your mother what she means to you and linger at the dinner table and have another piece of pie and talk about your day and why you and Susan broke up (again!) or how practice went? Wouldn't you like to see her eyes light up and hear her laugh and watch her talking with her friends or singing in the choir or teasing the bank teller or thanking the service station attendant or asking the sales lady at Rich's about her granddaughter? Don't you long to feel her gentleness and kindness and friendliness penetrate their lonely little lives, transforming their otherwise boring existence into something special and memorable and fun?

Don't you miss her for all of that? I do. And I'm still mad as hell that I can't have her back. She's the lucky one, escaping this cesspool of phonies and pretenders.

Even when we were kids, Lilly made my life and my world better. Mostly she made sure I didn't get in trouble with Mr. Bates. I detested the way he was always bragging about his kids, showing off, talking about how the Lord was taking care of us. Always holding court, always having the last word whether it was at your dad's store or over at the Iron Skillet eating breakfast with his deacon buddies.

He would've never lasted as a regular pastor at the same church every Sunday. They'd get wise to him. That's why he travels and does revivals all the time, outrunning his critics. I've heard those same five sermons five thousand times. I wanted to puke when he came home all puffed up, complaining about the honorarium he was given. It was only a matter of time before he would see Randall and start screaming at him. The only thing that seemed to calm him down were his private talks with Lilly.

I guess I was only two or three years old when I first remember that happening. She was reading *The Velveteen Rabbit* to me for about the third time that night when Mr. Bates came home, right when I was going to bed. When she heard his car pull up, she became distracted and wanted to hurry up and turn off my light. They'd go back into her bedroom for a while, and he'd come out a little nicer and a lot calmer. I have no idea what they talked about. It always seemed to upset her because she came out red-faced and very sad, sometimes crying a little. I know you felt bad when you saw her crying sometimes. It wasn't your fault. It was just something she needed to do every once in a while.

I've dumped on you without mercy, Jonathan. You don't deserve any of this ranting and raving. Please forgive me. I'm just so frustrated and my anger allows me to cope. I see too much. I see too many problems and not enough solutions. Ours isn't the only relationship that has been knocked off balance lately. I'm willing to admit to you that Janie and I are struggling, but you knew that. There's nothing more infuriating than another person's confessing my own sins. If only I had some idea what to do, which direction to go, I could handle things better. The only answer I know of is to keep putting one foot in front of the other and keep looking for the light. I hope we'll both find it soon.

Love,

S

Letter 7

June 3, 1965

Dear Graduate,

I know it's bittersweet to graduate from high school at long last with a full ride to Vanderbilt—but not to play football. Unfortunately, people will consider you a spoiled child for any perceived lack of exuberance over becoming valedictorian of your class. Those who haven't been through what you're facing have no idea. Don't expect anyone but me to understand the mixed emotions you're feeling now. I've walked that road myself. I know you can't easily turn loose of a lifetime of dreams and expectations.

Your biggest dream definitely hangs in the balance. Will you accept Vandy's invitation to be a walk-on this fall with only a fair possibility of earning a football scholarship? It may be that nothing you can do will convince them your knee will fully recover. Only a couple of the coaches you've heard from—the Citadel and Furman—seem confident you'll be back to full steam, and as smaller schools they're not exactly at the top of your wish list. Of course the honest truth is that none of us knows what will happen. The human knee was not designed for a lateral blow from some 250-pound tackler running full tilt. It was a legal hit, but oh my,

Jonathan, how you've suffered physically, spiritually, and every other way in the wake of that fateful second.

I can console you up to a certain point. I've never gotten over how suddenly and brutally my career ended at Tech. I know what it feels like to have the thing you've been living for most of your life blow up in your face. To see the foundation of your life ripped away.

Your biggest test may have been watching Buck getting courted by all the big schools—something we thought was clearly in your future before last season. How many offers did he finally get? Some obscene number. His dad told me it was between twenty-five and thirty. For your sake, I'm glad he decided on Tennessee and turned down Georgia Tech. I think it would have been tough watching your best friend playing on Saturdays at "your" school. I am still pissed that you got completely snubbed by Georgia and Florida. But how can we be anything but happy that your best friend has accomplished everything he and his family had been pursuing? Like I said, the whole deal is bittersweet.

And it's not as if you were completely ignored. The coaches at Alabama and Tech were completely sincere, Jonathan. They wanted you to come—even live in the athletic dorm—and see what happens. They want you to make it. They love your grit and smarts and winning attitude. I realize that playing football at Vanderbilt was never your dream, but you're making a good decision to accept the scholarship. It's the best kind of safety net if for some reason football doesn't figure into your future.

I also think you're making a good decision about spending the summer in Nashville. Janie and I will drive up to see you after you get settled. You'll be able to focus on your weights and learning the system at Vandy, and get to know some of the players. It will be a good way to transition from high school to college ball. I have no doubts about you, Jonathan, but there will be a question mark in their minds until you take that first hit and prove that your speed and toughness are the same.

Besides, how could they not invite you to come? Those coaches have been watching you for three years. You've been under a magnifying glass ever since that piece appeared in *Sports Illustrated.* I've read that little paragraph a thousand times. I couldn't have written it better:

"Faces in the Crowd"

Sports Illustrated, November 28, 1962

Jonathan Goodson

Pine Ridge, Georgia - Football

> Jonathan, a sophomore at Pine Ridge High, rushed for 231 yards and 4 TDs in a 45-28 win over Jessup Christian in the Class A state semifinals. He ran for 1,827 yards for the season, making him the first sophomore named to the All-State Team in Georgia high school history.

The Izod shirt looked great on you last week at Maureen and JJ's. Janie knew you'd rather have clothes than the gift I picked out, so we got you both. I expect it will be a while before you learn to appreciate the picture of C.S. Lewis. I won't be offended if you leave it at home. He obviously doesn't have the same appeal as the Beatles or the Rolling Stones. Even so, what a great conversation piece—a tweedy Cambridge don hanging on your wall next to the Fab Four and Mick Jagger's tongue. But then, he was technically part of the British Invasion wasn't he? I must ask you again how many times you've read *The Chronicles of Narnia.* Three was my last count. I think you're hooked on the guy. Which is good.

We bought that print in December 1963, only two weeks after Lewis died, an event that went completely unnoticed because it was the same day President Kennedy was assassinated. Heaven knew before any of us I'm sure, and that's all that matters. My humor is a little sick but I have the feeling that when Lewis arrived at the Pearly Gates there was something of a celebration; then when JFK showed up a little later the angels looked at him and said, "Who is this guy?" We on planet earth esteem things a little differently than those running the affairs of heaven.

The world is always changing, Jonathan. People like Lewis and Kennedy come in for a season and then they're gone. The same thing happens to each of us on an individual scale. You've graduated with highest honors from Pine Ridge and are headed for new adventures at Vandy. Everything changes. New relationships form, old relationships are reshaped. That leads me to something I don't think I would have had the courage to bring up on my own. But since you've been brave enough to take the initiative, I'm going to jump right into the deep end.

You seem very confused and concerned about your relationship with Buck Gordon's mother. And you should be. There's no question that this family has embraced you like no other. You've become a real son to them, even went with them on vacation to California last summer as I recall. Buck's dad has supported you from day one and Teri is beautiful, fun, and loving in so many ways. She absolutely reminds me of your mother. And she has filled up the empty space left by Lilly's death far better than your stepmother. The Gordon house has been a wonderful retreat from the chaos and unhappiness that seems to follow Helen everywhere she goes.

Here's the deal, Jonathan. The Gordons have become your substitute family. They welcomed and nurtured you when your own family couldn't or wouldn't. Helen will never come close to being any kind of mother to you. It's just not in her. She's consumed with herself to the point of mental illness and has no time or capacity for you. And what about your dad? He has done the best he knew how, but with Lilly dying and Helen blowing into his life like a cyclone, he's had nowhere to rest and heal. He couldn't go to the Gordons for refuge, so he opened three new hardware stores and got lost in his work. In running from Helen, he unknowingly ran from you.

It's funny how you and I start to talk about something that's bothering us and we just dance around the subject, like a plane almost out of fuel circles looking for a place to land. You've landed at last on the topic of Buck's mom, said what you needed to say and gotten real honest. That took courage and a ton of maturity. I'm proud of you and respect you for it more than you know. Above all else, Jonathan, there's no question of your integrity or sincerity.

Nothing you told me came close to being a surprise. Your relationship with Teri, though a blessing in so many ways, has been a ticking bomb in other ways. Since you've practically lived at their house these last couple of years, it was just a matter of time before an embarrassing moment would occur. The things you've been describing were bound to happen. The alarm went off, however, when I realized these incidents were occurring too often to be accidents, and were increasingly flagrant and inappropriate.

The last time involved Teri's watching TV with you in her silk pajamas—"silk pajamas" was what set off the alarm bells for me. An oversized flannel nightgown would have painted a completely different picture. And before that, she left her bedroom door open while changing her clothes knowing full well you were only a few feet away in Buck's room. Is that the behavior of a circumspect, responsible, modest, mature wife and mother? I think not. Provocative and intentional is more like it.

My own personal experience persuades me that this behavior is not innocent nor accidental. A year or so ago I arrived at the Gordon house to take you somewhere. While I sat waiting for you, Teri came in to greet me—in her swimsuit. More out of it than in, actually. She turned around and asked me to fasten her in back and apply her sun tan lotion.

Part of me wanted to stay and oblige the lady and see where this was going, and part of me wanted to run. So I compromised: I zipped up her suit, thinking, *So this is what it's like to be James Bond!*, and then made up some lame excuse about needing to go out to my car. I walked away—briskly, thank you very much—flushed and sweating, hotter than a firecracker. I was trembling and thought my heart would explode in my chest. I had to sit in my car for a few minutes, catch my breath and let the blood drain from my body. One part in particular, if you get my drift.

Jonathan, this woman is sensational. Did you know she was a cheerleader at the University of Florida and was the 1946 homecoming queen? She's still gorgeous and sexy and—this is the part that concerns me—seems to know it full well and use it to her advantage. A year ago I would not have been so frank. I noticed her then, but thought what I was seeing simply came out of my own fantasies and dark side. I'm only unloading today because it appears that "things" have escalated. Your friends are clueless: don't fret about what they're thinking. They're so obsessed with their own problems none of them would let their minds chase the idea that you and their friend's mother would be physically attracted to each other. "How disgusting!" they'd groan.

I, however, am not that naïve.

Teri obviously thrives on attention. It's her oxygen. Mr. Gordon knows this on some level but he could care less. I think he is disgusted and embarrassed over her childishness and self-absorption. I also think he is bored. Maybe he has been frustrated to the point of giving up on some facets of their relationship. Maybe he got the notion he couldn't measure up. Maybe he couldn't. It may be that, for whatever reason, he's become completely satisfied with his collection of *Playboy* magazines that you and Buck found under his recliner last summer. If that's the case, Teri will feel compelled to get some kind of validation the only way she knows how.

Even if she were blind, Teri has some animal instinct that knows when heads are turning her way, especially yours. And that, Jonathan, is my real concern. Some line has been crossed, and she's finding that certain needs in her life can be—and will be—met by you. Something in me wants to give you a warning, but I'm afraid you'd think I was judging you in some way. It might feel like shame or condemnation, or like you've caused all of this. Or that you're only a helpless young boy—which you are not—and therefore need someone to protect you from the evil women in this world. If I've come across that way then I am truly sorry. You, of all people, know that I'm not throwing stones at you or Teri or anyone. (My apology is only half-hearted, however, since you did ask.)

We are human, and our God-given needs and longings can get painfully jumbled at times. You know about me and my own vulnerability and guilt with women. The crucial difference between you and me on that point is that those girls were my age. Teri is thirty-nine and, lest we forget, married to your best friend's father. I know from experience how the reality of facts and details can be dulled, even obliterated, from our minds when lust—especially when mixed with alcohol—takes control of our lives. This is a case of emotions run amuck. But the stakes are much higher than two teenagers fooling around in the back seat of a car. Teri is on some kind of hormonal juggernaut and seems stuck emotionally somewhere between nineteen and twenty-five years of age. And that's being kind.

She isn't sinister or evil, she's only desperate for attention and, I believe, struggling with an addiction that sometimes manifests itself in terms of this animal attraction to hunky teenage boys. She can do a lot of harm to herself and others in this condition. I'm reminded of the passage in Proverbs 5 that says the lips of the forbidden woman drip honey but her steps follow the path to hell. I don't want you to get stung, Jonathan. Or worse.

We will continue this conversation.

Yours faithfully,

Saul

Letter 8

April 21, 1966

Dearest Jonathan,

I'm so sorry that playing football at Vanderbilt didn't work out for you. Who could have predicted that after all the work you did rehabbing the knee and adding back the muscle and weight you lost over the summer that you would get mono! Dr. Rutgers said it was one of the worse cases he's ever treated. You barely moved for a month. I'm glad we could be there for you and you were willing to stay with Janie and me.

We were very impressed with your new friend Tim Blake. One of the times he came to visit, you were so out of it I don't think you ever even knew he was there. He seemed so genuine and gentle. And he obviously thinks a lot of you, since he made sure you got connected with his little sister, Gina. So there you were, bumping along getting ready for football season—which you believe God knew was never going to happen—and you meet this incredible athlete and spiritually sensitive guy who steps in and gives your life a whole new direction.

The most satisfying moments in life seem to come when we're in the presence of someone like that: honest, easy to talk to, whose only agenda at the moment is to be with us. We usually blow right past those people because we're so unaccustomed to someone truly listening and caring. I can see why you were attracted to him. He's just the kind of person to open a door to a new life for you, Jonathan.

For all your interest in Tim these days, you seem taken even more with the man who's been mentoring him, Grayson Weller. I understand completely. It takes a unique person with a unique approach to get through to college-age people. His appeal to them is striking. He has the gift of taking those old themes and sermons we've heard at Little River Church a thousand times and transforming them into incredibly attractive reasons for becoming a more deeply committed Christian.

I actually met Grayson and heard him speak several years ago when I was playing at Tech. Coach Wilson felt the team needed some motivation and a boost in morale, so he invited this young minister to lead us in a chapel service before a game with South Carolina. Grayson talked about God's love and forgiveness in a way I had never heard before. He blew us away. Everyone was expecting the usual little pep talk: let's be better people and more focused baseball players, dear God don't let us get hurt. That didn't happen. In fact, the whole thing was far more than Coach Wilson had bargained for. Grayson never came to the locker room again.

I'm a rather superficial person, so it doesn't surprise me that the first thing I noticed about Grayson was how great he always looks. Just like you, he destroys every stereotype of the Christian nerd: an athletic, charming, articulate package wrapped in cashmere V-necks and Weejuns—no socks, please! God has gifted the man with wisdom beyond his years. What I caught most, however, was his passion for the students. He truly has the heart of a teacher. Great sense of humor, too. Janie and I are tempted to drive up every Thursday evening to hear him—and to see you, of course.

I'm afraid I was and remain one of those people who got vaccinated with just enough of the Christianity thing to make sure I never got the real disease. It's always been hard for me to separate what I saw and experienced with my father from the kind of real-life truth Grayson was talking about that day before the South Carolina game. But I've thought about it a lot since then.

When I went to Cambridge I started hearing the same message again—in more academic, more theological terms, of course— and it really made sense. For years I've said there's got to be more to the Christian faith, but I've never really pursued it. Yet the questions keep hanging around, and I sometimes feel the stirrings of change in me.

You're changing inside, too, Jonathan. I'm not sure how it started, whether it was when you met Tim Blake and Gina, or when you started listening to Grayson Weller. By the time you came to live with Janie and me this summer, I knew something was up with you, and it wasn't just because you had mono and a high fever. Our talks were different. You were asking questions I couldn't answer. You were subdued and reflective.

We thought you were possibly depressed at having to face the awful reality that football was no longer in your future. I remember when you were finally sitting up in bed and started talking about that day you spent in your dorm room completely alone. I think it was Labor Day—what irony. It was the day you cried for the first time since your mother's funeral, the day you actually prayed and asked God to help you. You described it as something like opening your heart to God. Your sincerity touched me, and I thought, *There's something quite real going on here*. Some of it sounded like Lewis' description of his own conversion to Christianity—how a number of factors seem to come together at the same time, so that the whole idea of turning one's life over to God actually made excellent sense, almost logical. Though Lewis was never as riveting and entertaining as

Grayson, he was deeply profound and compelling in discussing his faith.

By the way, I hope you have forgiven me for my off-handed comments over the holidays about your finding a Girl, a Guru and God to take the place of The Game. I'm sure it was the "lemonade" I'd been drinking. I thought the alliteration was quite good, even if it was sarcastic and demeaning. You handled yourself well as always, and remained loving and kind toward me in my less-than-coherent state.

I like Gina very, very much. You'll be astonished to hear I believe her best quality is not her commitment to Jesus Christ, but that she thinks you are the complete stud. She adores you, Jonathan. That kind of devotion to you compels me to love and accept her completely. Janie kept saying on the way home, "They are perfect for each other!"

Gina is vibrant, beautiful and well-spoken, though at times I feel as if she's straining to figure out your relationship to me and how you came to embrace someone with so many personal problems and struggles. I don't know what to think about that assessment. You know me and you know my heart. But since she does not, I will extend to her the right to feel that way about me. Many of my personal habits apparently contradict the idea that I could be a serious follower of Jesus Christ. I smoke every chance I get, drink too much at times, say the "s" word often, and have always had a miserable relationship with my father. But you know that those things serve as my cover, my tried and proven way of dealing with my own shit (oops!) and thus not letting people get too close to me even though I love them and desperately want them to love me. If she got any closer, there would be no doubt in her mind that I'm going straight to hell and that Janie is a saint for living with me. Don't give up on me, Jonathan. Please.

I know you won't, and that's one of the reasons you'll make a good preacher. Janie and I enjoyed seeing you and Gina in Nashville last week, to see you so confident that God is leading you to go into the ministry when you finish Vanderbilt. I love your passion and enthusiasm these days. I haven't seen that kind of focus and intensity since the beginning of your senior year, before you hurt your knee. The light is back in your eyes and I am most grateful for that.

There was a time when I was maybe eight or nine years old that something like what you've been describing may have happened to me. This was a time in my life when I so much worshipped and believed in my father. I saw him as infallible, perfect, strong and true. I didn't have a place to put his failures and inconsistencies as a man and as a father—in other words, his humanness. I needed him to be everything that's good and loving and all-wise even though he was not.

When he was harsh or mean to me, I felt that it was because of something I had done, some kind of flaw he saw in me. That's when I felt empty and alone—not some of the time, but all of the time. So I tried opening my heart to God (at least this is what I was told I was doing). What followed was an Encounter with Something larger and stronger than me, Something protective and caring, Something forgiving and accepting, Something that brought me some bit of peace and happiness. But it (He?) vanished as quickly as it had appeared. Later on, I immersed myself in baseball and dating and parties. I successfully shut down some soft, vulnerable place within me and pulled a shell around me, shutting out God as I came to understand Him as much as I knew how.

The result is that today I am clueless and cynical. Indifferent. I have no idea how to break open this thick shell of defensiveness and no desire to do so. My rejection isn't based on some intellectual argument about the truthfulness of Christianity. It's just a complete disconnect for me to even go there: to me it's bullshit. That's how I've managed to navigate my own little world of relationships, my own confusion and disappointments and sadness and anger. You know I'm still trapped in my anger about quitting baseball, I'm still wallowing in loneliness over losing Lilly—my sister and my mother, my best and only friend other than you. I'm disillusioned with my expectations about marriage. Quite frankly, Jonathan, the best thing I can say to you in your spiritual quest is this: Good for you; enjoy the ride; I sincerely wish for you all the best in your pursuit of Jesus and the good life and Gina and this new arena in which you will be performing.

And, yes, Jonathan, Mr. Bates (that title has helped me keep him at a safe distance, you must understand) does have lung cancer. Thank you very much for visiting him. Yes, I am afraid that he will die soon; yes, it's true that I don't know what to say to him; and yes, I will be the one who will at some point soon begin to take care of him and watch over him in his remaining weeks and months, something I desperately want to do and also something I intensely hate to even think about.

Your father called unexpectedly last week and told me two things that were troubling. First, he said he had not heard from you in over a month. He graciously chalked up your non-communication to the fact that you are totally in love with Gina and no one else exists in your world. He is very understanding, or perhaps he's just protecting himself from the fact that the two of you have so little to say to each other, especially when Helen's around.

The second little tidbit may be of interest to you in a sort of morbid way—that he and Helen now have separate bedrooms. Possibly he is coming to the realization that the woman he married to fill the void after Lilly died is nuts. It wouldn't hurt if you called him every once in a while.

Tell Gina and Tim hello. We'll see you in two weeks.

Love always,

Saul

Letter 9

October 14, 1968

Dear Jonathan,

It's late, almost midnight. Janie and I just got back from Tallahassee where we were visiting some McCallie graduates at Florida State. Though I'm dog tired after driving ten hours, you've been on my mind since we were together last weekend. Janie insisted that I come to bed, but I've been writing this letter in my head for the last three hours. Now's the time to dump it on paper.

This is the first trip she and I have taken together since she moved back in last month. We had originally agreed to separate for three months, but she asked to come back after only six weeks. Her attitude is so much better. I haven't sorted out everything—my feelings for her, what needs to happen now. But I'm going along with our counselor's recommendations, and he's encouraged us to start fresh and take things slowly. "One day at a time," he chants. We are both pretty raw. I'll give you the details in person at Thanksgiving.

I wanted to thank you and Gina for praying for Janie and me. We really need it. I'm actually beginning to believe that praying may make a difference. The clincher was watching your grandfather's cancer go into remission. He was really touched by your repeated visits and praying with him in the hospital. You have a great gift with your words, especially when it comes to encouraging people and making them feel loved.

I believe another factor that shortened Janie's and my separation is my agreeing to go to Alcoholics Anonymous. I haven't had a drink in over four weeks. This is something I can do to show good faith—that I'm working on myself and trying to forgive us both for the mess we've created. I know I need to make a lot of changes whether we stay together or not. But it's a real pain going to all of those meetings. We meet at a little church in Chattanooga, so the whole evening including drive time takes almost three hours.

The best part for me is talking with some of the men afterwards and hearing their stories. I've made friends with one man maybe ten years older than I am who is a well-known doctor in Chattanooga. Another guy I've come to like a lot—you'll find this interesting—is a Baptist preacher! Both of these men have been going to meetings for ten years or more.

You had some questions for me about the background and teachings of Alcoholics Anonymous. The people do talk about God or a "Higher Power." But I can't really tell you if it's based on the Bible or Christ or whatever you were asking. We say the Lord's Prayer at every meeting. I can tell you this: it's not like church and for me that's a good thing. Going to these meetings and talking with the counselor are two things I need to do for a while. I've told Janie that I am willing to give it six months.

It's still hard for me to believe that my little nephew Jonathan is getting married after Christmas. I'm curious about the struggles you've shared with me as the big day approaches. I want to be sympathetic, but I'm having a hard time understanding. The last couple of times we met, all you wanted to talk about was your physical relationship with Gina. It makes sense to me that you would want to be together every chance, but that seems to be part of the pressure you're feeling.

In those first conversations, Grayson Weller's influence clearly weighed heavy in your mind, particularly his insistence that you and Gina keep your relationship "pure," which I take to mean no sex before marriage. That's a high standard for anyone, Jonathan, and in some ways I'm wondering why you would even discuss it with me since you know my past is anything but snow white.

But there's something in you that is honest and sincere about this desire and the commitment you and Gina share. So far, according to you, it's been a tough road but you're making it, with only two months to go before your wedding. I think you said that "technically" you and Gina have not had sex. I won't prod you for details.

The frustration you expressed to me has been enormous, eclipsed only by a huge load of guilt because even though you and Gina have never had intercourse, you've...well...you know exactly what I'm referring to. The guilt and shame of it hang around you like a wet blanket, even though when you talk about Gina there's nothing but happiness and joy about being together. And you talk of all this gratitude for "how the Lord has brought the two of you together," as you say.

The other part of our discussion that concerns me is your sense of—I don't know how to put it exactly—doing all of this for God. I get the sense that your sexual relationship is a bargaining chip for you and Gina and the future of your marriage. I hear the same theme coming from her. She's incredibly intent about obeying the Bible and honoring God, but mostly I pick up an attitude of righteous indignation toward others who don't hold to her standards about premarital sex.

Correct me if I'm wrong, but I think I'm hearing you say you feel that whether or not God blesses your marriage down the road depends on your sexual self-control between now and the wedding. The flip side I hear is that if you and Gina do in fact "save" yourselves now, God will be more inclined to bless your marriage in the years ahead. That's where I get the idea of your sexual purity as a bargaining chip between you and God for the future. "Purity" can be a relative term in itself—I'm not real smart when it comes quoting Scripture—so perhaps God will grade the two of you on the curve. Maybe Grayson could fill me in on the merits and accuracy of my understanding. I'm sure Gina would be glad to enlighten me, as she seems to think she has it all figured out.

Knowing you and your heart, Jonathan, I see something good coming from this desire to be the man, the husband and someday the father that you believe God wants you to be. That's such a decent and commendable quest. It's a longing that seems always to have been there, compelling you to believe your life would be different, committed to a higher standard—a life aimed at changing people for their own good and helping them in their relationship with God. Am I right?

Part of me is very proud of you for setting such a standard, but another part wants to pull you out of this pressure cooker. What am I missing? I don't understand why you and Gina are so uptight about all of this. What happened to just having fun and enjoying each other? It's like each of you has forgotten the individual you fell in love with in the first place and are all caught up in this perfect Christian couple thing. Don't misread me here. I'm not recommending that you simply live together, but sometimes I wonder whether you're more excited about her or about this idealized vision of a perfect Christian marriage.

This is something I've seen in you over the years, this quest to be more than a regular guy, certainly above average, maybe even superhuman. I'm assuming from our discussion that you've discovered the temptations and failings of humanity are well below the standards you first took on for yourself. That shouldn't surprise either of us. You know how your mother always put so much pressure on herself to do the right thing. That trait seems to have been passed onto you, along with all the good stuff in your mother. Your dad has always been more relaxed about things, at least outwardly.

The older I get, the more obvious it becomes that our parents, whether we liked them or not, shaped so much of who we are and who we become. We don't talk that much about them, but they are with us or in us forever. They leave their mark, and we end up living out their attitudes and values whether we believed in them or not. That is so weird.

I've completely lost track of what I'm trying to say. The salient point is that something about the simplicity of two people loving each other seems lost. What's left is a grinding out the remaining days of pre-marital boot camp until at last you are married and have complete permission to hop into bed and go crazy. How does a couple go in one day from being all uptight and serious and holy (whatever that means) to having wild sex and enjoying every minute of it without reservation?

I've thought a lot about this. Especially since Janie and I have been having so many problems. It seems to me that there are basically two kinds of people with two different approaches to life, which are often revealed in the way couples relate to each other in marriage, or in your case, in the relationship you and Gina now have. The first kind of people are those of us who want very much to get things right. We want to get life right. I think this is you, Jonathan, and probably me too. I think you want very much, with God's help, to have a great marriage, and on some level you feel that's it's up to you to make that happen—that by doing certain things consistently and with the proper motivation, your relationship will come together and have the fulfillment, as you would say, that God and Scripture always intended.

Getting it right has always been your quest. That's why even as a boy you knew that if your mom was happy, life was going to be better for everyone, especially yourself. Every child, young or old, feels this omnipotence in being able to shape the happiness of the significant people in his or her life. For young children of course, that means their parents. The satisfaction of making them happy is one of the most wonderful feelings they ever experience.

The problem with longing to get it right all the time is that it makes you completely dependent upon others going along with your idea of what "getting it right" looks like. Most people could care less: they're groping in the dark like the rest of us. And, so we getting-it-righters are left to search endlessly for that someone special who is willing to say, "Way to go,

Jonathan, I believe you got it right!" Then we can feel okay, a little more secure, a little more sure of ourselves.

Our whole lives are understood in terms of this quest to get it right. It's the quest that defines us—to have that sense of worthiness—not actually getting it right. And who's to know when we do get it right anyway?

I meet a lot of the parents at McCallie, most of whom are well-to-do and run in the more affluent social circles. They belong to all the right clubs and churches and civic organizations. They've made it to the top financially. Yet they live with this constant pressure to get it right. The women carry the biggest burdens to look good and dress according to protocol for their girlfriends. I used to think they dressed for their husbands, but I was wrong. Every minute, they look for confirmation that they're wearing the right clothes, saying the right words, getting their kids into the right schools, putting in time at the right charities. There are a thousand different ways they can be okay or not okay depending on the circle they run in. They desperately want assurance that their peers think they're getting it right.

I remember Mr. Bates railing against these people and the "liberal" churches they attended, calling them down for their materialism and their love of money. "Worldliness," he called it. What a strange word. Some of these folks are the most generous and giving people I've ever met. At times I get the impression from them that deep down they can't stand the relentless pressure to look perfect and do the right thing, whatever that is. But they don't know how to get off that treadmill.

Here's my point: some of the most devout Christians or religious people I know are just as bogged down with doing the right things and appearing righteous and perfect as the socialites who are accused of living for the world. I don't see any difference. The motivation and shame and guilt look the same for everyone. One group says, "If I get it right for these people, then I'll be okay and approved and accepted into the circle." Another group says, "If I get it right for God and these people (i.e. live a pure life sexually), then I will be okay and approved and accepted as a faithful follower of Jesus Christ." In a way, they're both looking for a kind of "blessing" as a reward for doing the right thing, whatever the group decides is okay. It takes someone or some group to give that final validation.

What would become of our striving and longing it we actually did get it right? It's an impossible quest.

And that impossibility introduces the second set of people: those whose goal is not to strive to get it right, but who are convinced they're already right and that their job is to set everybody else straight. Usually the first set is intimately connected to the second. One set measures success in terms of how hard they fight to get it right, while the other gauges success according to how right they are, which is pretty damn right. Either way, it's a matter of survival. That's why, ironically, we strivers usually end up attracted to people who are less inclined to give us the validation we want, to finally tell us that we "got it right." It insures we'll always have something to strive for, thus some way to measure success. To feel worthy.

What about those who have to be right? Any relationship will do because to them no one, including you, Jonathan, will ever really get it right. There will always be something about us that falls short, something that's defective, something incomplete about our endless and futile attempts to get it right.

That brings me back to this concern and quest you seem to have about the purity of your physical relationship with Gina. You want to get it right. You want God to bless your relationship because you have successfully "saved" yourselves for marriage. As I've heard Grayson say in a variety of ways, I thought we were to save ourselves not for marriage or the future but for God himself. This kind of thinking sets up a promise or guarantee that the rest of life, messy and grossly unpredictable, will be right. In other words, this focus on doing or not doing one thing is like a house of cards. If one card, sexual purity, falls from its place, the whole house of cards—the prospects for a fulfilling and prosperous marriage—comes crashing down.

Gina, of course, is not the one in your relationship whose purpose is to strive at getting it right. That role is way too demanding for her; it falls exclusively to you. Gina is the keeper of the gate who lets you know when you get it right. Her role in life—hers, yours, and others I'm sure—is to be right, to analyze, judge, indict and sometimes condemn. Very rarely condemn, but the threat is always there. She represents the standard, the biblical viewpoint she would hope to be. I think your position and hers are equally flawed. Who's worthy anyway? Who decides? And who cares?

On to less complicated and more enjoyable matters. I guess we'll be seeing each other at Thanksgiving. Randall told Janie that even he and his family are coming up from Macon. They're hoping to see you and finally meet Gina since they're not going to San Antonio for the wedding after Christmas. Mr. Bates called and he also wants to see you and Gina again. He is really excited about your decision to go into the ministry. Your dad was able to convince Helen to have his former father-in-law come for the day. I'm thinking this whole thing will be okay. It's been seven years since Lilly died and Jess and Helen got married. Some of the drama and tension has subsided, but the politeness is as superficial and phony as ever.

You've probably heard that JJ and Maureen will not be coming to your wedding. It's a bit pricey for her and a long drive for JJ. They'll join Janie and me at Maureen's on Saturday after Thanksgiving to eat leftovers and watch the Georgia-Georgia Tech game.

I think it's fantastic that Buck gets to be in your wedding. I'm sure he had mixed feelings about wanting to be with you, and is certainly disappointed that Tennessee won't be going to a bowl this year. His mom is coming with him. *That* will be interesting. Have you seen her recently? That whole deal seems like a lifetime ago.

One last thing. I was glad to hear that on your last visit to see your grandfather you took Gina by your mom's grave. What was that like for you, and for Gina? It's impossible for me to go to Atlanta without driving by the cemetery. The groundskeepers think I work there. It's just one of the ways I try to stay in touch with my better self—the place is sacred to me. I feel at peace and more secure after spending a few minutes there. Lilly talks to me. It reminds me of the feelings I had as a kid when I'd play by myself down by the creek. Getting quiet and still is next to impossible for me these days. But going to the creek then, and now to Lilly's grave, the quiet and the stillness fall on me like a cozy patchwork quilt. There's no other place that does it for me. It filters out all of the noise in my life, all my fears and worries, and everything gets to be okay for a while.

I may have to go there more often, Jonathan. Life's getting crazier and lonelier. Teaching and coaching are great distractions and keep me focused for a few hours. But at the end of each day my life feels pointless and empty. Your advice to me does not fall completely on deaf ears. What you say is good and encouraging. I've just not found the routine or structure or disciplines in my life to pray every day or—I like the way you express it—spend time with God and His Word. Ken, the doctor I met at AA, tells me to get on my knees every morning and surrender my life to God as I understand Him—just for that day. It seems to help, when I remember. But I'm just so inconsistent. I am really pathetic when it comes to God and doing the religious bit. For some, like you and Gina, reading the Bible and all of that comes so easily.

Seeing you two will be great. I can't wait for Thanksgiving to get here.

Call me soon.

Love,

Saul

Letter 10

April 4, 1973

Dear Jonathan,

I so hoped things would turn out differently for us.

I have a deep sense of loss. My sadness comes back in waves when I least expect it. This morning I was thinking, "None of this can be happening!" That you had to be mistaken in believing God has led you to end our relationship.

After you drove so far to speak with me, I knew it would be best to wait and let some of the emotions settle down before I called you. I can't ever remember a meeting like that before. I was such a jerk, yelling and saying things I will regret for the rest of my life.

Yet I was certain we could somehow forgive each other, re-connect and start again. We always have. But not this time. It's been three weeks now, and the bond between us shows no sign of restoration. There's been a fracture.

I've never been so confused and ashamed. I veer back and forth between feeling hopeless and empty, then going off in a fit of rage—not at you, but at the insanity of our situation. You were emphatic that this was just between you and me, but I don't see it that way. I hear Gina's voice behind your words. I feel her energy propelling you along.

It was probably best that you left Gina at home when you came. Having said that, I have no doubt that something in you is feeding off her contempt for me. It seems that your closeness to her, combined with your natural inclination to avoid conflict through appeasement, has influenced you a great deal in this. What I don't think you see is that at any moment she can turn her death ray of disapproval and contempt on somebody else, including you.

You've been in Gina's cross-hairs before. Because of your tenderness toward her and because you're so keen on keeping the peace, I suspect you don't fully sound out your own true feelings. You insist on calling those poison-tipped arrows of hers "spiritual discernment" or "honesty." You love this woman for good cause: she is passionate and she beautifully complements your longing to touch people's lives. Like you, she has a way with words. I only wish she weren't so hurtful with them at times.

I don't know if she told you that I called last Monday. It felt like the right thing to do at the time, and I didn't intend to be intrusive or disrespectful of your feelings in any way. But it's obvious to me now that I did cross a line. For that I apologize. It's just that I've been groping around in the dark trying to find my way back to you. So far that effort has proven fruitless. I am completely shut out.

To her credit, when Gina took my call she didn't water down your resolve. She made no attempt to protect my feelings by saying you weren't available, or that you were busy or out of town. She just told me straight out that you have made the prayerful—and final— decision not to see me or speak with me again. And that was that.

I'm writing to you today to share my thoughts and some of my feelings. It will be my last letter, no doubt, as I do intend to respect your decision and new boundaries. I can't be sure that you will ever even read it, but that's all right. This exercise is mostly for me, in hopes of getting some clarity on all of this. Most of all I feel sad. I haven't slept for several days.

I want to put something down that will distance me from the constant anguish. Even more important, I want to be sure you know that I'm sorry, Jonathan, for letting you down. And I want to say how much I love you. You mean more than anything to me. I know I'm rambling here, but that's because I really don't know what to do or say.

I know I've failed to live up to your expectations these last couple of years. Unfortunately, most of my standards have remained the same while yours have changed in significant ways. You apparently were able to overlook some areas of my life, like the smoking and drinking. I think you gave up on my swearing years ago.

My guess is that what finally pushed you over the edge was my decision to leave Janie. Our discussions about Christian marriage have been frequent and intense over the past year, and you've taught me so much during those times together. It's clear to me that in your view divorce is never an option. I still have the letter you wrote to me last spring, along with your seminary paper, "Divorce and Remarriage."

I can't really come up with a "biblical" reason for my decision to get a divorce. Certainly not one that would satisfy you or Gina. However I do agree with you that divorce is always "a miscarriage of marriage." I like the way you put that, and it's surely true for Janie and me. We have no one to blame but ourselves for the breakdown in our lives and the disintegration of our love for each other. Somewhere in that little book, *A Severe Mercy*, Lewis' friend Sheldon Vanauken asked something like, "What's behind the failure of love?" His answer is simple: "creeping separateness." That's Janie and me.

We felt so close at one time, but now we can only talk about our estrangement and how painfully aware we are of how little we ever actually knew about each other. I do think when a person gets married, his or her commitment is to an idealized vision of their marriage partner, not the real person. That's what makes the whole thing like rolling the dice. I know you disagree here, but I digress.

Frankly, when you and I started talking about my marital troubles I hadn't even thought about specific biblical justifications ("grounds" was your word) for ending our marriage. I didn't know such proofs existed until I read your paper. The bottom line is that I have no reason for divorcing Janie that you would consider acceptable. I do have my reasons, but I can't say they are good ones or why they've sent me down this lonely road. I sincerely believe that staying in this marriage would be harmful to both Janie and me—perhaps life-threatening. But then you or Grayson or one of your professors would remind me that God can heal a marriage as broken as ours. We can ask for a miracle. To which I would respond, "I am finished with all the asking."

You're right that there's nothing good about divorce. Similarly, I can't think of a single thing good about a terminal illness. We pray to save a marriage, we pray to save a life. But the time finally comes when all the hoping and praying are done and the only thing left to do is pull the plug. Children and spouses and parents do it every day. Maybe they don't have the faith that God can heal their dying sister or father or mother, or maybe they've grown weary waiting for a miracle. The very idea of ending someone's life is dreadful. But they do it anyway, in spite of the lingering doubt and the horrible guilt that clings to them.

Gina has already reminded me more than once that a miracle has taken place in my case: Janie does not want a divorce and is willing to work things out. On the surface, that puts me in an untenable position as the defiant partner. I've had lots of experience with Janie taking that approach over the years. Now, as they say, the shoe is on the other foot. The sad truth is that I'm sure my resistance to Janie's overture at reconciliation is what has led both of you to give up all hope for me and consequently, directed you to sever personal ties with your Uncle Saul. How did Gina explain it to Jess? "Saul is unrepentant!" I can just hear her spitting out those damning words. I'm not sure what all that really means, but it sounds terrible.

Even though you disagree with what I've done, I trust that you realize this decision is mine alone and has come after literally years of agony, confusion, frustration and, as strange as it may seem to you, many hours of prayer. I'm not comfortable discussing any more details other than the fact that, as you know, Janie and I have struggled for the longest time. It's not that I'm hiding anything. But I do not have the freedom to share with the two of you the intimacies of our marriage. Whatever she chooses to disclose to you or Gina will be up to her.

One thing I sincerely hope you and Gina will not do is blame my involvement with Alcoholics Anonymous for this decision. They have not brainwashed me. They have made it quite clear that their acceptance of me, regardless of what happens between Janie and me, is unconditional and complete. They do not judge me, and they're certainly not kicking me out of the AA fellowship because of my divorce.

In a recent meeting, I was awarded a "chip" for not drinking for two years—a true miracle. Ironically, two years ago I would have been in no condition to make a decision to leave Janie. On the contrary, I would have been terrified of the idea and could have found your biblical argument to stay with Janie no matter what a convenient "out." It would have been a safer and easier place to live. Staying required little of me in terms of personal responsibility, accepting life on its own terms, facing my fears of conflict with Janie or, of course, disappointing you. Now it appears I've not only disappointed you, I've lost you.

Without my bottle, I am forced to my knees every day. No one in AA has counseled me, as some have suggested, to do whatever makes me happy. That's the very kind of thing my friends and my AA sponsor would challenge me on. They would say I'm running from my problems.

So many people (I meet most of them at church) hold on to this distortion of AA, or maybe it's just a sincere misunderstanding. AA does not promote doing what makes a person happy. It encourages rigorous personal honesty, something I have longed for my entire life and which I've discovered is not nearly as easy as I thought it would be. Alcoholics Anonymous is not a cult, Jonathan, and has no interest in undermining or diluting the tenets of Christianity.

The Scriptures are referenced in meetings from time to time. Parts of the Bible that I've heard my entire life are starting to make sense for the first time. It's moments like these that I wish my understanding of the Bible was better because from the little I've read, I get the sense that loving people and forgiving them often is the main thing being taught. This particularly includes loving and forgiving ourselves.

I'm still the amateur in all of this, Jonathan. It's easy to defer to you and I usually do. I respect your perspective and wisdom. So I must ask you: Am I missing the point when it comes to the teaching of the Bible, or what Lewis called "mere Christianity"? Love has been the mark of our friendship from the day you were born. And now this development.

Never have I heard more clear and life-related presentations of God's grace, compassion and tenderness than when I've heard you teach. I will always remember your lessons on Paul's letter to the Galatians. With that in mind, what you're doing now just doesn't make sense to me in any way, not only because of how you are attempting to apply the Bible's teaching on divorce to my life, but also because it's so out of character for you. You seem so willing to judge and make a clean break with someone who, though horribly imperfect, loves you and wants the very best for you. I'm wondering what Lilly would be thinking about all of this. Actually, I'm not wondering. Your mother would side with me in that none of this begins to fit the Jonathan we have always known.

This is a good place to stop. Even though it represents a kind of ending, what's inside of me will continue, Jonathan. I know that on some level you will never leave me. The place you fill up in my heart will always be yours. We are growing and changing and learning. More often than not, that process is confusing and painful. As I said at the beginning, I wish more than anything that this whole thing had never happened.

I will respect your choices. You are no less in God's hand today (nor am I) than the day you were born, or the moment we both lost Lilly. Any future day in our lives rests equally in His providential care, however beautiful or, God forbid, dark and hopeless. I'm sounding like you now.

You are the one who has taught me all of this about His mercy: that we are forgiven people and He has brought it all about. Nothing from us. Everything from Him. God will never love us any more than He does right now, or any less, no matter what. And though my love for you falls short of His, I will always love you and I will always be here for you.

Always, Jonathan, my door will be open. No matter what.

Ever faithful,

Saul

Journal Entry 2

1987

Journal Entry 2

June 8, 1987

The meeting on the Monday after my world exploded was another massive jolt. I guess I was still in denial. I knew that their decision would be harsh and limiting, but I had no warning about the punishment that was coming down.

Naïvely, I was hoping the next session would be my first step on the road back to normalcy, the counselor's way of telling me how and when I could move back into my duties as a pastor—all clearly spelled out over some appropriate and structured time frame.

What failed to register with me was that the first meeting had been my trial, an open-and-shut case where I was swiftly found guilty. The next meeting, I soon discovered, was to be the sentencing. The first thing out of their mouths was that no formal legal charges were being filed at this time. So I thought, "This is a good start."

But then, with Gina sitting next to me, I heard as one voice the people in Barbara's office demanding that I step down from my position at the church immediately. There would no time for goodbyes, farewell receptions or stopping by the office to pack up. I was locked out of everything. All of my books, personal files, diplomas and pictures showed up a week later in thirty-three boxes neatly stacked in my garage.

They were emphatic—underlining every guideline and boundary—that I was not to do any speaking, teaching, or counseling. This council of five—Barbara, Alexa's lawyer and three elders from my church—also said that they would be monitoring my activity and watching me closely for the next two years. Any real or perceived violation of these restrictions would immediately bring the filing of formal charges. I would not be permitted to officiate at any of the weddings already scheduled for the summer. No preaching at any funerals—not even offering a prayer at the graveside service of a long-time friend and church member who had died that week.

The only life I'd ever known was over.

It's been a month now since my wife and kids drove to San Antonio. It was a surgical move on Gina's part—two days after school ended, they were gone. We had agreed together to pitch the trip idea to Lilly, Blake and Grayson as an extended vacation to their grandparents' lake house, while Daddy stayed behind for personal study. Their return date was left open-ended.

Gina has not been returning any of my calls, and I've talked to the boys only once, on their birthday, as they were running out the door. All three children seem to know what's going on. There is an unmistakable distance between us. I'm angry and feel cheated by Gina that I was never given a chance to tell them my story, as grim and devastating it would be, and to ask my children in my own voice to forgive me for destroying their lives.

Two months of severance pay from the church comes to an end this week. Then, no more money. I've mailed my one-page resume to several potential employers—selling insurance, fund-raising for non-profit organizations, even telemarketing—but no one wants to hire and train a forty-year-old man with four years of theology, Bible and New Testament Greek. I am considering an offer from a Vanderbilt classmate who owns a huge landscaping business, but eight dollars an hour won't go very far.

I can't call my Dad—not with Helen listening in the background. Everywhere I go, every person I meet is loving and friendly, but my fear of rejection and embarrassment hold me back from seeking their counsel and help. They apparently haven't gotten the word that I'm a womanizing, home-wrecking adulterer.

I'm not sleeping much either—staring into the dark for much of the night. That twisting knot in my stomach comes back in waves now, but with the same intense, wrenching pain. Walking at Percy Warner Park pushes the anguish and panic into the background, but only for a while. Praying feels like a waste of time. Nothing seems to help. I'm desperate and terrified of what's coming.

Yesterday was another Sunday morning alone in my big, empty house. Eating a bowl of cereal and sipping orange juice, I found myself staring blankly at the Bible across from me on the kitchen table. The fear, the anger and despair, seemed to rise up from inside me all at once. I exploded. I snatched up the Bible and, in a fit of rage, started swearing and tearing at the pages, ripping them out a hundred at a time, twisting and mauling them into a thousand tiny pieces.

This was my treasured Bible, the one with all my notes from seminary and personal study—the one I had used in sermons and classes and counseling for almost twenty years. When I was done, I sat there lifeless in the chair, spent, exhausted. All that remained were stubs and chunks of torn paper sticking out of the leather cover with my initials gold embossed on the front, and piles of confetti scattered across the kitchen table.

As my head stopped spinning I was surprised to feel a sense of incredible relief. The boil had been lanced, at least for the time being. Suddenly I couldn't bear the thought of sitting in that room another minute. Moping and worrying and wringing my hands weren't going to get me anywhere.

Minutes later I was buttoning my shirt and putting on a blazer and tie. For some mysterious reason, I decided to go to church. It would be my first time since preaching what turned out to be my last sermon. My destination that morning was a quaint, 80-member Episcopal church an hour's drive south of Nashville—a place where I was sure no one would know me.

I took the freeway out of town, then turned onto a two-lane road that took me deep into the country, past open fields and horse farms. So peaceful and serene. About halfway there, I pulled over onto the gravel shoulder and stopped, but left the engine running. The air conditioner blew full force into my face.

I leaned my body over the steering wheel and stared through the windshield, my nose inches from the glass. Cars and trucks moved back and forth through the intersection ahead like some mindless silent movie. I started shaking. Sweat poured down my face and neck, soaking my starched white shirt.

It was then, in that place, Sunday morning on the shoulder of a country road, that a profound sadness fell upon me. I started talking and praying out loud with my eyes wide open.

"Oh, God," I sighed, "my life is a disaster. I can't fix it. I don't know where to start, and I can't get any traction." The tears came in a flood. "I've lost my kids, Lord, I've trashed my family. And now my heart is so cold! I hate Gina for not calling. Nothing's working."

I thought about my Bible, its shards and gold-stamped carcass still lying on the kitchen table.

"God. Jesus. Oh, Jesus, please help me! I'm so sorry. I am so sorry. Please do something, will you? Please, Jesus, I beg you, help me, Lord."

Along with the tears, there was a heaviness and emptiness, the kind that comes when the doctor tells you it's cancer and there's nothing you can do. "There is no hope. You best get your affairs in order."

Trance-like, I saw out of the corner of my mind's eye familiar words streaming in front of me, like electronic letters wrapping around a building in Times Square—very familiar words, often comforting words.

The sacrifices of God are a broken spirit.
A broken and contrite heart, O God, you will not despise.

I started repeating these words out loud like a prayer, and underneath the words something suddenly shifted in my spirit. My heart was breaking as I thought about my kids, but to my surprise, I wasn't feeling guilt or judgment or shame or any of those things I had been dreading. I didn't feel the knot in the pit of my stomach pulling tighter as I'd expected.

I felt the presence of what I think was Kindness—the sense that something good was about to happen. Then came the realization that I was the one person responsible for this moment. Suddenly I could see everything displayed before me with sober, crystal clarity. All of this was *my* doing. My sin and selfishness had brought all this sadness and tragedy on me and my family. All the deception, the pretense, the living in denial—all my own doing. I had used a precious woman. I had slept with another man's wife—my friend's wife. My choices had fueled all the chaos, all the confusion and bewilderment. Of course, Gina would leave. Why would anyone want to live with me?

Now I just needed to take care of my family.

The fog was lifting.

The knot in my stomach relaxed completely for the first time in weeks. I felt alert and clear-headed. I sat up, put the car in gear and eased into traffic. I made a left turn at the intersection and headed for St. John's.

There were no more streaming words, no more strange feelings. No more confusion. I knew what to do.

Letters

1987-1989

Letter 11

June 15, 1987

My Precious Jonathan,

I'm so glad you turned off your car before it was too late. Ending your life that way would have been too horrible to imagine for everyone left behind who loves you. I'm asking you to come stay with us for a while. Come today. I want to see you and give you a place to rest and talk—or be quiet. You're suffering terribly right now. I'm a bit selfish about that, about wanting you here. I can't wait to see you.

I've missed you every day for fourteen years and I'm ready for my suffering to end. Please, Jonathan, just come. We have a room for you. You'll have your privacy, but you won't be alone.

I know you're worried about Gina and the kids. I know they left for San Antonio a month ago and haven't called now in several days. They will, Jonathan. They will contact you when they're ready. What you want from Gina is not going to happen. The reassurance of her love and devotion to you. As desperate as you are to have it, that is a gift she cannot give you right now.

Gina is confused, angry and full of fear. Let her be in that place for the time being. There is nothing, no person—especially Gina—who can ease your anguish. Nothing. It's called suffering, Jonathan. The most critical thing right now is to be still. To rest and be as close as possible to the people who will support and love you. It's like drowning, Jonathan. I can hear your gasping and grasping for hope.

In times like these, we need food and we need a safe place. Don't forget to eat. When you come, we'll take some long walks together like we used to. All we can do is to let the helplessness wash over us. Our natural tendencies make us desperate to fix everything immediately, this very minute. We rush around looking for reassurance, some sign that all will be well. We want to stop the bleeding, feel in control and find a way out of the mess.

That's why we act out. It's complete insanity. We want to medicate our pain. In my case, my brain tells me that things will be better if I have a drink. Now that's really brilliant. That's why I want a drink—even today—to end my suffering. But the suffering and the shame that follow are worse than the problem that pushes us. Quick fixes only make things so much worse. I've learned to wait and accept the suffering. So I'm not suffering as much, and I'm not drinking.

I won't tell you that suffering is good for you, that it will make something of you. I can't make that promise. All I know is that accepting where you are now will get you through it faster than trying to fix it or make it go away.

The loyalty you feel toward your family and the ministry is as strong as ever. You're clinging to all that you've ever known. It's a familiar world, one that has served you as much as you have served the people in it. I know you feel the water rising and the fear along with it.

I hate confusion as much as you do. I can almost hear the wheels turning. What's next? What shall I do? How will I provide for my family? Where will the kids go to school? Where will the money come from? All of these things probably do fall on you and you alone, but you are not capable of sorting it out right now. Not today, not even this week. Let the confusion be what it is. Let the raw feelings and misunderstandings, all the accusations and defensiveness, rattle around for a while.

And what about your relationship with Alexa? You mentioned that you want to sort that out. It seems strange to talk about it, but I think we must. Besides all the devastation in your family and humiliation with your friends, there's Alexa. What are you to do about her? I find it interesting how emotions and guilt and shame and all the crappy feelings we know about can run along with each other, even when they don't seem to belong in the same conversation.

You feel an emptiness toward Alexa where once there was a dear friendship, now twisted and abused and lost forever. At the core, it was a relationship between two people who sincerely cared about each other, but they forgot their boundaries and lost their way. No one intends to have an affair. None of us looks for ways to destroy our credibility and betray the people we love the most. But it happens every day. It's happened to me, and now to you. We made those choices, Jonathan.

What have Jeff (isn't that her husband's name?) and his friends done since everything blew up? I wonder how she broke the news to them.

If we've been living in the shadows—and there are many ways to do that—the first reaction to any light is to hide our faces, minimize the consequences and deflect an accuser's condemnation. It's all about survival. Damage control.

We can forget the worn cliché that the truth sets people free. Not at first. Not in every circumstance and every life. Maybe never. It depends. For a long time, facing and accepting only a fraction of reality is unbearable. It takes time to tell the truth, much less accept it. But if we tell our stories often enough again and again with people who love us and accept us, if we remain rigorously honest, we will eventually start telling the truth to ourselves. And about ourselves, our hearts and our lives. Then a new kind of freedom creeps into our lives. It just takes so much time.

King David hit the same wall you have. Psalm 51 was probably not written the very day Nathan confronted David over his adulterous affair with Bathsheba. I suspect months passed before David was able to own and embrace the weight and responsibility of his destructive and self-absorbing choices. Our first impulse is not to become transparent by revealing the truth, but instead to cover our actions and minimize the cold, hard facts. You are not alone in this. We're wired to run and hide. Fear has us by the balls. And here's the crazy part: we actually start begging the people we have wounded to restore our balance and sense of security.

Most affairs trace a similar trajectory to a similar end. First comes the downplay of any affection for the person who for months has felt our undying love and commitment, the one person we actually believed made our sad lives worth living. Then we feel repulsion toward this secret lover bordering on disgust. Is this not disgust at ourselves for getting caught or for even going down that path in the first place? It's all very strange and twisted.

Of course it was just a huge mistake: it was merely sex. But it didn't "just happen." Rarely do we find someone caught in an affair coming clean: "You know, you're right. The passion was great and I do love this person, and so, I'm done with my family!" That's why I'm encouraging you to do nothing. If that's not possible, then say nothing. No one is going to believe a word you say anyway. We're not very credible or coherent during these times.

Good decisions are impossible with this much emotion, shame and confusion swirling around. The best thing to do is nothing, except to the extent that underneath the deadness of your spirit you can hear yourself say, "I will take my time and try to do the next right thing just for today." Eat three square meals, take some walks, go to the bathroom, pray, sleep if you can, take a shower. Start over the next day. The fog will start to lift—a little.

I would start by *not* calling Gina again. Give her the space she has insisted on, along with a good bit of time. You have zero credibility with her right now. I know you heard her at the beginning condemn and blame Alexa for the affair. But again, that was her unconscious attempt to minimize the possibility that you could have chosen someone over her. Gina has lost a good friend too. Two of her closest friends have betrayed her.

Gina knows it takes two people. We all do. We all feel a bit awkward with the idea that the flawed partner in a fit of lust walked away from the flawless spouse for no legitimate reason. It's not that clean and simple, even though we feel better if we can simply point to the guilty party. Hell, we're all guilty.

She feels betrayed—mainly by you, Jonathan. She has come up short because you, in spite of your overtures of commitment, found her lacking, said by your actions that she was not quite enough. That's intolerable for anyone. In response, she opts for anger instead of sadness. She feels safer with her anger. All her life, anger and rage and blame have been her best friends when it comes to surviving, because sadness is too much of an admission that she might be part of the problem. It makes life too vulnerable to bear.

We know—not at a heart level, only from the neck up—that no human being is ever going to be enough. No one can fill us up. That's not what a marriage is for. These days I wonder what marriage is about, wonder even about God's intentions for two people coming together. He knows that we are broken and empty—theologians describe this condition as "fallen"— and that we are seldom if ever inclined to pursue Him with our whole heart. We can't actually see and feel Him. All we really know is trying to make things work on our own. What are we to do but find substitutes for Him to keep ourselves going for a while, attaching ourselves to someone or some thing to sedate our nagging insecurities? A deep, sure sense of security is not the normal state of our lives but rather a fleeting and elusive anomaly.

I love your honesty, Jonathan, even though you tend to push yourself down. I've often wondered why we do that, talking about how guilty and worthless we've been. Is there some twisted consolation that comes out of telling ourselves that we're beyond hope? This reaction is not humility, that's for sure. It's the flip side of humility, actually, a kind of false pride. "Look how bad I am!" This is self-absorption run amuck.

In AA we talk about our terminal uniqueness, the idea that no one has ever been down this road before, just me. I'm the only one who has ever had this happen to him. Poor me. We all go there from time to time. It makes sense that you have joined this particular pity party, the bandwagon of self-bashing. But I know you, Jonathan. You will not stay there forever.

Your honesty and transparency are refreshing. We have all made a mess of our lives, not just you. Every life is a mess. I'm still recalling the people I have hurt. Some, not all of them, I have tried to make amends with: reputations I have torched with slander and gossip; relationships I have wrecked with disloyalty, name-dropping and self-promotion. So many have I misled and used! It's only been in the last two or three years I have been able to look at all the people I have harmed without minimizing any of my responsibility.

Days before my father died, I finally found my way to his bedside. And we talked. Neither of us was as defensive as I expected. It was rich, it was real, and we found each other ready to forgive and be forgiven. I asked him to forgive me for never giving him a chance to be in my life, and mostly for the years I spent trying to discount his Christianity and expose to others the inconsistencies in his life.

You know better than anyone how I have hated this man. I tried to blame him for every unhappiness and frustration, every episode of depression, for my alcoholism and failed marriages. He was so handy. He's always been such an easy target. Now things are different. Every broken relationship, every drink I've ever taken I can now trace back not to what he did or didn't do to me, but to my own bitterness and resentment toward him. I know this may seem unbelievable in light of the long list of his failures and shortcomings. The fact is that forgiveness sometimes seems unbelievable. Certainly Christ's forgiveness of us is. I don't pretend to understand it, but that's what I feel and I'm very grateful to be in that place.

I had never heard it before and I don't know where it came from. But before I left that day, my father actually said that he was sorry. He said he loved me and Lilly and Randall. Jonathan, I believed him.

What's left is a sadness that resurfaces again and again for all the years I missed with him—so many wasted years—along with a wonderful joy and relief in knowing that we did finally return to each other. I am spared the burden of regret and shame that would have hounded me to this day for never risking his rejection one more time. I'm not even sure how it all came about. Looking back, I see myself being carried in a sense to a place of reconciliation, not knowing that making peace with my father was probably written into my life from the beginning. Perhaps that was God doing for me what I couldn't do for myself.

Speaking of messes, I clearly recall the time when you were almost two years old, which would have made me twelve, and you discovered one of those black magic markers on the kitchen table. I was supposed to be watching you, but I was glued to a baseball game on TV. Lilly walked into the house and the next thing I heard was, "Oh, my gosh!" You, my friend, had scrawled your first work of art on the new hardwood floors and kitchen cabinets.

Lilly was Lilly. In the calmest of voices, she said to me, "Let's clean up this mess." The cabinets required a fresh coat of paint, but we salvaged her much-loved floors with a whole bottle of nail polish remover and a roll of toilet paper. Not less than eight times did I say, "Lilly, I am so sorry. This is my fault." She never corrected my assessment of the situation, but when it was all done she put one hand on each my shoulders, looked into my guilty face and said, "Saul, it's okay. We all make messes. It's okay."

In spite of my disdain for my father, in spite of my cynicism toward the church and the Bible, I got a dose of grace that day that I have never been able to shake. She planted in my heart in that moment the possibility that there is a God who would love me unconditionally.

We all make messes, Jonathan. It takes a long time for most of us to understand that in the days following the messes we created, we are still loved.

I went to two AA meetings today, one this morning before my first class and another on the way home after work. I shared with the men and women how happy I was to have this very special person back in my life, but so sad about his profound losses and confusion. Not only sad, but feeling very empty and powerless over his situation.

That's what all of this rambling is about. I'm just trying to make sense of something that is so far removed from anything I can control or solve. All that I know for sure at this moment is that I want to see you, Jonathan, and wrap my arms around you. I know that it will feel like I've come home when we see each other.

Come as soon as possible. I'm anxious for you to meet Lindsay. We've been married for six years. She has been the greatest gift in my life—until today, when I heard your voice again.

All my love,

Saul

Letter 12

September 3, 1987

Dear Jonathan,

Randall, my big brother, died. It's been almost a week now. Marcie called me in a panic last Friday around 1:30 in the afternoon. Something bad had happened. "Probably a heart attack," she said. Fifteen minutes later she called back. "He's gone, Saul. He's gone." The the next eighteen hours were a blur—I cried throughout most of the night.

"Randall is dead." I've said it out loud and written it down. I see it on the page in front of me, but it still hasn't registered. I'll go through more stages of anger and acceptance as the days move along. First Lilly was gone, then my father, now my big brother. The family that was once so real and vibrant and influential is melting away into the past. My own death seems more imminent and less theoretical than ever.

Today also marks another year of sobriety. Fifteen years without a drink. I'll wait a little longer to pick up my chip. Maybe next week. I'm not much in the mood to celebrate anything, and certainly not in a mind to share with the fellowship "how I did it." Whenever someone gets an anniversary chip, everyone starts chanting, "How'd you do it?"

I'm kind of amazed myself that I've been sober fifteen years. Sobriety has probably contributed more than anything else to the healing in so many other areas, especially my relationships with Lindsay, my father, and Randall. The greatest evidence is having you back in my life. My heart is seemingly at rest, knowing I'm in the care of God. (I bet you're shocked to hear those words coming from me.)

I think something happened in my life when I was a young teenager. You know that story and how I blew it off as a kind of religious phase, a spiritual infatuation. It was a wacky, dysfunctional, messy ride after that. Now I understand a little better. It's only from my perspective that I appear to have "found" Christ. The fact is that He revealed Himself to me over time, and you have been a prime influence in that unfolding. He was within and around me from the beginning.

I have not stayed on the path, not by a long shot. Yet throughout the journey He has simply kept drawing me to Himself, freeing me along the way from my misconceptions, bitterness and pride.

I am not only sad, but very confused—disturbed and getting a bit angry—about the timing of my brother's death. We were both hoping to live out much of our remaining years in deepening and growing friendship. Marcie and Lindsay had become close as well.

I don't know how we can do that now. Maybe in heaven later on. For now, he is with others up there, free of his health issues and that terrible addiction to nicotine. And free of his bitterness toward our father and the ghosts of the abuse he endured as a child. Truly, he is freer than I am at this moment. He is dancing and singing and talking with others freely and openly, which was not Randall's style. I hope he is able to experience all that really matters. We talked about this just last month.

My hot tea tasted exceptionally good this morning. Maybe I'm just more aware of my feelings and sensations. Along with those good feelings, I am frustrated and miserable. I don't know how I can manage not having Randall only a phone call away.

Lindsay and I went shopping yesterday, and while paying for a pair of slacks at Macy's I struck up a conversation with an elderly gentleman waiting next to me. I started telling him about how I had lost my big brother, that he was only sixty-eight, that he was a great guy and loved people and his family. The old man, probably close to eighty, was gracious and smiled while I rambled on. I wanted him to know that I had a big brother who really loved me and taught me important stuff and that I missed him very much.

That said, some of Randall's glory is fading a bit. He left a big mess: little money for Marcie, unpaid and unfiled back taxes, a ton of debt. He and my dad never made up, never found a way to lay aside their differences. It would have been way too much for our father to admit his abuse and slanderous remarks. Maybe they will patch things up in heaven. I don't know how all of that works; understanding heaven eludes me. I know that God is good and that He loves me, but that's about as far as I can get into the mystery of what happens after somebody He loves dies and goes to be with Him. I know the words and phrases and what is supposed to be said, but I'm not sure if I believe any of it.

At this point you're probably saying to yourself, "What the hell is Saul talking about, all this closeness with a brother he hardly spoke to over the years?" This healing between Randall and me came only four or five years ago, right after Lindsay and I were married. It's an interesting thing how all of this turned out. Lindsay didn't have any of the old baggage and feelings toward anybody in our family. I'd been sober for four years when we started dating, so I was a lot less toxic and the venom that normally spewed from my mouth was more subdued. From day one Lindsay thought Randall was a neat guy, totally loved the way he and Marcie had raised their kids and told them so. I saw my stiff, frozen brother melt before my very eyes under Lindsay's warmth.

Love does that kind of thing, Jonathan. Disarms people, and enables them to lower their own defenses without their even thinking it through. Their hearts say something like, "You know, this feels like a safe place. Maybe I could relax, drop my guard and just be myself."

Where is he now? Where are you, Randall? I still hear your voice in my head. I saved your last message on the answering machine. Yesterday, I hit the wrong button and now you're gone—again. Where are you? I need to talk with you. That's what we did once we reconnected thanks to Lindsay. We talked. We didn't solve many problems, but we talked. We complained, we tried to fix each other, we tried to be right all the time, but mostly we just talked. I miss hearing, "This is your big brother. Call me." I would if I could, but I can't. Surely you know this. So please stop saying that same phrase in my head over and over and over. "This is your big brother. Call me." I get nauseous. I want to throw up. Mostly I'm sad and so I cry, Randall. I can see you, I can hear you, but not really. When I saw you in the casket, that's when I really got angry, screaming and cussing like a crazy man. Where are you? We had a lot more to talk about, Randall. I can't have our conversations by myself.

Randall is gone, Jonathan, which makes me even more grateful that you're still here. Still living, still hurting. If we're hurting that means we're alive, and as long as we're alive, we have hope. One more time I want tell you how much it meant to me having you at Randall's memorial service. His going away has left several holes, not just the brother slot. He was also a fantastic and very loyal friend and, of course, a constant mentor.

So, there are many holes I'm feeling every day. Mainly I just miss the talking, miss hearing his voice. There was a freshness about his voice. I'm not sure he was a great listener. He was like a parent in that regard, liked to tell me what to do. But the overall memory was that I knew I was safe with Randall. He was my big brother. Now he's gone, our sister's gone, our parents are gone, and that leaves me next in line.

Randall is dead, I am alive. I hurt, he doesn't. I have hope, he has peace.

Yours faithfully,
Saul

Letter 13

December 14, 1987

Dear Jonathan,

Your despair has lessened a bit. The dark clouds are parting and a little sunlight is peaking through. This is good. It's something I have found can't be forced, much less predicted. We think God moves too slowly, but He is unfailingly gracious in offering relief just when we think we can't go another hour, another minute. Maybe He wants us never to forget how much we need Him. I'm not sure why this relief has come to you now, except that you've given yourself some time to step back from the trauma that has shaken your world to its foundation.

Maybe it's a good thing that after a while, we survivors find it easy to minimize the worst things imaginable happening in our lives. The first skill we learn is to cope. Only later do we look back and wonder, "How did I survive all that?" If we saw it all ahead of us on the front end, I don't think we could go on. I suppose God set it up that way so that we could eventually gather the self-awareness and courage to live in the reality before us instead of running from it. If I've learned anything, I've learned that following Jesus means accepting reality as much as I can, accepting life on its own terms. I'm getting better at it, but it's always been easier to talk about it than to actually do it.

Some of us lean more toward pessimism, which I do at times, while others refuse to see any gloom or serious problems anywhere ever. *They* are the ones who bother me, especially the ever-sunny religious crowd. Their talk is so empty and tedious and predictable that it puts me in a bad mood just being around them. The desperate cheeriness they have on display brings me down, because I strongly suspect it's nothing but a smoke screen of lies that they tell themselves in order to make it through their own messy and difficult problems. I find them toxic. These are confused and wounded people whom I believe Jesus needs to save from themselves—and save me from them too while He's at it.

What has happened to you is a kind of death. And there will be others. One of the first things I recall "dying" in my life were my dreams of playing professional baseball. In the broader scheme, worse things have unfolded in my life than not getting to pitch for the Cubs. But at that time it meant a complete meltdown. The world I knew, the world built around the assurance that I would play ball, had come to an end. There are days I still feel sad about it, but not for long.

I've learned to accept the fact that life is a series of deaths along the way. Some big, some not so big. But in the heat of the moment, in the absence of maturity and perspective, every one of them seems huge and life threatening.

I hear some acceptance of that in you, and that's good. Acceptance is critically important. It seems to be the hinge our whole lives turn upon. It can determine whether we will have happiness—moving forward toward some sense of purpose and meaning—or whether we plow through life as victims, waiting in vain for things to work out or watching helpless as the next big dream turns to dust in our hands.

I couldn't move forward until I accepted the fact that I was an alcoholic, that I was powerless over the bottle, that my life was a mess and completely out of control. My alcoholism affected everything. In a veiled sort of way, I remember hearing you and Grayson and others teach about our spiritual bankruptcy, our inability to earn God's love and approval. That it was not until we "declared bankruptcy" that we could understand the life God had for us. The problem with that teaching, however, is that it's only a theory until we hit a very real-world bottom and see that our life choices have put us on the path to disaster.

I hear the sadness in your words, in your voice, when talking about your children. It's a good sadness, but one you cannot burden them with. They carry no responsibility for the breakdown of your marriage. That's a train wreck only you and Gina will be accountable for.

Those precious kids—the losses they suffer, the friendships they must give up, the routine and safety and comfort they will never know because two so-called adults had just enough tools to be dangerous to others in making life all about themselves. We're so hopelessly empty, so needy, so determined and demanding in our spirits in getting what we think are our needs fully met. We can't handle the unhappiness. We can't stand the boredom. We can't wait on the loneliness or emptiness to be medicated through sex or food or busyness or booze. It's always about getting what we want *right now*.

The children meanwhile are just along for the ride: trusting, helpless, completely dependent on the ways and thoughts and willfulness of their broken and wounded mothers and fathers. They have no choice. Later they will have choices, but then it's too late. They've already been scarred, disapproved, unloved, set aside and left to struggle for the rest of their lives with what love is all about, how to navigate and solve problems without hurting the people around them, some day their own kids.

Hurting people hurt other people. And the people they hurt, hurt people. Then those hurt people hurt people. And so it goes. We take it and we pass it on, endlessly repeating the cycle. Is there any alternative? I wonder.

You can see that I'm frustrated this morning, Jonathan, and it's not all about the plight of neglected children. I walk past the old racquetball gear in my closet almost every day. And almost every day, I hear that deep sigh, the breath leaving my body, reminding me that I can't go there any more. I once played singles and doubles for hours at a time. After three knee surgeries, those days are gone. For a few seconds, I feel the sadness move through me and then it's over. I believe that jolt of grief is about more than racquetball. It carries the accumulated losses of a lifetime, the thousand other deaths I've experienced.

The first losses I think are some of our dreams. The things we anticipate, like going fishing with my father when I was nine years old, then watching him completely forget the promise of driving to the lake together on Friday after school.

For a whole week I lay awake at night, too excited to sleep. Dad and I would be roughing it in the woods for a day, sitting side by side on a fallen log, eating our ham sandwiches and Ding Dongs in complete silence—him watching me, showing me how to hook a worm and throw a line into the water. I didn't know that he knew as much about fishing as I did; as far as I was concerned, he was the smartest, most powerful person in the world. And out of everything he could have been doing, he chose to be with me!

Then none of it happens. He forgets, or maybe he never intended to follow through. Either way, my dream is shattered and I feel ashamed (em-bare-assed) for wanting something from him so much. I feel stupid and exposed and flawed. And, we never talk about it. He never mentions it again. Ever. I start hating myself. That hate and disgust, I discover, has served me well in playing down the repeated disappointments and losses. "It's no big deal" became my mantra. I was always lying.

Broken promises and shattered dreams come in all sizes. Those hits on the heart multiply quickly when we're growing up. Most of them are small, not life-threatening, but they teach us ways to survive the hurts and insults we experience as adults. Unhealthy ways. Isolating ways. Numbing the sadness that comes with failing at anything or of feeling abandoned, unwanted or just left out.

Few of your dreams had died at the time in our lives we both lost your mother. Those deaths came later—the dreams of living large and accomplishing something great. Feeling like we really were making a difference.

Outwardly, very little changed at first. It was almost as if Lilly had never died, or worse, as if she had never lived. We simply merged back into life's fast lane and went on our different ways, desperately hoping the loss and sadness wouldn't catch up with us. Blood of our blood, flesh of our flesh, ashes to ashes, dust to dust, mourned for a day, buried under an attractive marble grave marker and prayed over for seventeen seconds by a Baptist minister. Anonymous workmen shoveled the red clay on top of the casket with a hollow, clattering sound, filling the hole where Lillian Bates Goodson's body would rest forever. We shuffled back to our cars, drove home, huddled around the TV with aunts and uncles and cousins watching *The Honeymooners* and eating pound cake.

The next day, I lay in bed exhausted. Grief is exhausting. But I chalked it up to too little sleep and too much vodka. You went to the pep rally and heard a thousand teenagers scream when your name was announced as the youngest player on the Pine Ridge High School football team.

Your dad re-married a measly twelve weeks later. It was a kind of collective insanity. Life was back to normal.

We didn't talk. We couldn't. Not about Lilly. Not about the simple fact that she was gone. Because that would touch our sadness and push the pain to the surface. And we hate pain. God, how we hate to hurt and cry and feel that pain and anguish. The pain makes us feel so weak, so completely helpless.

We never learned how to cope with something like this. We cannot, we will not let it enter our lives, especially with another person watching us dissolve and weep and shake down to our bones. This was not merely losing a day in the woods with my dad, this was Lilly, precious Lilly, ripped from our lives. A tidal wave of loss.

This is the kind of stuff that has been working its way through me since we last talked, almost twenty years ago. In AA we call it recovery. Recovering our lives, our emotions, our capacity to be in relationship with ourselves, with God and others. So much of recovery requires good grieving, allowing ourselves to feel, likely for the first time, the holy sadness that accompanies any loss, any form of abandonment and shame. Then, usually to the accompaniment of many, many tears, we learn to grieve the months and years we have sacrificed in order to guard those secrets and pretend to be in control of our lives. We never were. As the secrets are exposed and the tears flow, I am being healed. I am finding my life. It seems to be happening to you too.

Blessed are the people who mourn.

Grief is work that must be done or the unfinished pieces still hidden will destroy us. At the very least, they will keep us sick and unclear as to what life is about. Failure to grieve is another way we keep secrets in our families. First, ignoring the little hurts we inflict on each other. Those wounds eventually become infected and they never heal. More wounding and more pain come. They must, because that's how life goes, how it works. Lots of wounding and a thousand little deaths and all of those subtle and not-so-subtle losses and hits on our fragile hearts.

It's not that we are soft or cowardly. When we gloss over or deny what happens, we are forced to act resilient and strong. We dare not reveal any signs of confusion or weakness. But it's all for show. It's what we think is expected of an adult. It's what causes the unhealed, unacknowledged wounded places to come out later—sideways, in fits of rage or depression or acting out, inflicting more pain on ourselves and the people we love the most.

We will always hate pain and sadness. We will always try to avoid weakness and feeling powerless. But they are the path to life.

Years ago, I heard a quote about life and following Jesus: "Pain plants the flag of reality in a rebellious heart." At first I thought it was pretty cheesy. Then I figured out it was a paraphrase of something Lewis had said. Today, I believe my old professor was on to something. What I'm not sure about is whether everybody who experiences pain has a rebellious heart or, if he is in rebellion, is ready to accept reality. But the potential is there.

It's something I'm watching firsthand in your life, Jonathan. It's a hard thing to come by, some sense of peace, a growing contentment with our wildly imperfect circumstances. I think it involves taking a long, hard look at not only the obvious mistakes and sins we have committed, but the deeper defects and motivations, the fears and longings, the ways we "decided" even as a child—later as a young adult—what it was going to take to make us feel safe, loved and validated in a very unsafe, unloving and shaming world.

Unconsciously we get what we need, do what we must do to shout down and shut out the unbearable reality; to create a world where we feel powerful, invincible and in control. It must be a very small world, one we can manage when we elect to be the master of our puny universe.

Our worlds have graciously been shattered, brought to their bitter end. Our kingdoms have been conquered and our virtual dynasties have come to a close. This, we discover at last, is how God blesses and enriches and fills our lives with all that was missing while we pranced about as little rulers.

Blessed are the poor in spirit.

One by one, the idols in our worlds are brought down, revealed for what they are—vapor, empty clouds, passing traditions and decaying possessions, yet more destructive than we ever imagined because we gave them such power. Through them we remained captive to falsehoods about ourselves and others, not to mention the Creator and Savior Himself.

And yet, even as the walls of our fortressed existence come crashing down one by one—the crushed expectation of playing a sport before adoring fans, the death of the people we thought would live forever, the abandonment of a spouse, the rejection of "best friends," complete financial reversal and suffocating debt, the bankruptcy of alcoholism, the humiliation among our peers—we STILL cling with an iron grip to the notion that we can rebuild this house of cards. We can be the comeback kid! We even have the unfathomable gall to pursue the re-building of our little kingdom on earth in the name of Jesus, asking Him to restore and rebuild not the lost intimacy He longs to share with us, but the flimsy structures of our frail and dying egos: recognition, financial security, social advancement and approval among our peers. Even a successful ministry.

There is nothing wrong with any of these accessories of life—and that's all they are—coming as gifts of grace. Though we cannot earn them, we have every right to enjoy them. Our proper desire is to be faithful, to surrender with all our hearts, a true willingness to be no one in particular.

That's when I feel the freest. An incredible honor we will one day cherish once all of our temporal toys and shallow expectations have been lovingly stripped away from our hearts leaving only us: the men God has always loved.

Yes, Jonathan, we are insane. We look for protection in everything except the One that will surely deliver us every time the darkness threatens and the arrows fly. God won't keep us from getting hurt. That's not His job. God will keep us from losing hope. And hope makes the world a different place.

Love,

Saul

Letter 14

May 4, 1988

Dear Jonathan,

I'm glad you had such a great visit with Maureen and JJ last week. At the same time, I understand your reluctance in seeking them out. Moving back into some of those relationships, especially the ones that were so intimate in our past, can be downright terrifying. The expectation for rejection is very high. All the anticipation and joy you once experienced with these people are replaced with apprehension, a sense of dread and a fear that they won't like you any more.

Because of the twists and turns your life has taken, your mind plays tricks on you. You're not sure these people even want to see the person you think they think you've become—the person who has failed to live up to their expectations, failed to be worthy of the admiration they once had for you.

It's all nonsense and part of the lies, part of the insanity we carry inside of us.

Every one of us is different now. None of us can remain who we once were. In some ways I never was that person to begin with. The real me was somewhere deep inside my public image under the protective layers of "personality" I had cultivated over the years to make myself more acceptable, more loveable; a composite image I made up that existed only in my head.

We have been so skilled at building a great, well-packaged persona, Jonathan. We're just now learning how to be the person we've always been, instead of the person we've pretended to be; how to be that person God has loved unconditionally from the beginning.

God loves *us*. Not who we think we are, and definitely not who others think we are. God loves me in the midst of every success and every failure, every defect, every addiction. He knows them all. Once I figure out who or what I am not, all that's left is me. And that's the person God loves and cares about.

JJ has loved you from the very beginning for who you are. I think you've always known this, Jonathan. In fact, he consistently does that better than anyone I've ever known. It seems to me that, beginning many years ago, JJ was planting a seed in our hearts that a mysterious kind of love was possible, a love that knows no bounds. When the time was right in our own lives, we finally started letting that love in.

Maybe you're getting an idea of what's been going on behind the scenes all these years when you decided to go "into a far country." When Gina packed up the kids and moved to San Antonio. When the elders of your church demanded your resignation.

However, as I believe you've begun to experience, what we think is the end of our lives actually turns out to be the beginning. When I got my third DUI arrest and had to come before McCallie's ethics council, that was without a doubt *the* worst day in my life. It was also one of the best, because it finally woke me up—literally brought me to my knees—to the truth that I was no match for my addiction to alcohol.

In everything up to our respective life-changing meltdowns, we were kind of sleep-walking, oblivious to the fact that our lives were a pretend thing. The word I'm looking for must be "pretense," a way of hiding, constantly figuring out what others wanted us to be, even needed us to be.

No one worked harder at it than you and I, Jonathan.

Now the idea of you and me living "pretentious" lives sounds a little judgmental to me, as if we woke up one morning and made the clever decision to pursue a fabricated, made-up, fake existence to intentionally mislead others. To live a charade. A lie. Our real motives remained hidden from us, but that's exactly what we were doing. We never consciously intended to mislead. But somewhere down the line, we must take responsibility for everything we do, conscious or not.

Our goal or purpose—actually it was more like a deep longing—was that they would truly like us. Most would agree that this is nothing less than an addiction, socially more acceptable but no less an addiction than my battles with alcohol or women or cigarettes.

After a genuine spiritual awakening, we can expect some relief from that compulsion to please others. We stop adapting all of our behavior to the expectations of those we most esteem—the men and (for me) the women whose acceptance and approval carry the greatest weight in determining our sense of belonging, of being somebody. Their opinions become the measure of our worth. They become our idols.

At our core, we are card-carrying idolaters driven by a legitimate, God-given longing to be loved and accepted.

When we talked about all of this last week, you described it as living in the dark. It's hardly living, but I understand what you mean. The Scripture says that we are not only in the dark, but actually dead. That whole idea reminds me of those black and white zombie movies where dead people stagger around throwing up their intestines and killing every living person they meet. They don't even know they are dead. They're clueless.

Hell, I looked alive. I thought I was alive and made a commotion as if I were alive everywhere I went.

I was clueless.

I was stumbling in the dark—a spiritual cadaver. My ignorance, the result of living as if everything depended upon me, was overshadowed only by my self-centered approach to life and the arrogant certainty that I was surely on the right path.

It can't get much darker than that. My ignorance and my arrogance fed on each other until I was ripe for slaughter, for bringing down a life: my own. I know now that it was God's mercy that let this floodgate of failure and despair run its course. He knew from the beginning what would happen, how long it would take, and how much pain I would tolerate. From His perspective, my journey back into His arms was never in question. He was confidently waiting, even when I was running from Him. Cursing Him.

We are the lucky ones, Jonathan. That's not a good word theologically, but it feels right for me. I am so damn lucky that God has done for me the unthinkable, the impossible. My best thoughts, my purest spiritual intentions, my most sincere and what I wished to call loving acts were the very things that hindered His tenderness and mercy from moving deeply into my life. My own delusion of goodness and sincerity sabotaged any possibility of something real with God.

The strange twist to all of this is that I believed even more defiantly in my own righteousness when I was drunk on booze or women or both. It's not only the "good" people who resist seeing their true need and spiritual bankruptcy. We all do. We all search first in ourselves for something good and acceptable—the bargaining chip for belonging, for being loved, for tipping the scale in our favor.

We're spiritual con men.

We live with a psychological safety net called denial that saves us daily from falling headlong into the abyss of rigorous honesty. We get glimpses of that truth. The curtain gets pulled back occasionally and we see the very real shadow side of our lives. Then in a moment of panic, we scurry to the safety of our relative righteousness ("Well, at least I'm not as bad as John!") and self-acquittal ("I know my intentions are sincere even if my choices are ugly!").

We bring nothing of our own to this equation, nothing to our story of healing and recovery. Not only that, we start with a deficit in the form of a long trail of shattered dreams and the broken hearts of people we promised to love but ultimately betrayed.

I speak this way with Lindsay from time to time. Like you, Jonathan, she can take me there to this place of speaking openly, looking honestly at what matters most to us, trying to better understand the journey we have begun, looking to God for everything. None of this has come easily for me.

When we slow down we have a better chance of connecting, really hearing each other. Yet slowing down is not only difficult, it can be very unsettling. It takes more than just doing nothing. The chatter continues in our head even when we make an attempt at some solitude or find a quiet place.

Most days, I feel that I'm on the road designed for my healing and recovery. But then, while on this good path, I discover another deeper, hidden place to drop into and be present with myself and someone else. And God.

You mentioned yourself about coming to an opening, a new place where things were a bit easier to understand and accept. Those times are so incredible. But they don't last for long. We want to make these times happen at our choosing, to have another spiritual experience show up because of our good behavior, because we have prayed or meditated on scripture or have been especially diligent working the Steps.

We want a formula to make it all work.

But we cannot manipulate or merit things in the spiritual life. We can't force our hearts open. We can only be willing. We cannot manage mystery. Those times come as pure gifts. Most of these times happen for me when I'm with that other safe person, like Lindsay or you.

Although I haven't quite learned how to turn the volume down on all the chatter inside, there have been times when, for no reason I can think of, there was a connection.

The magic returned.

It happened last night with Lindsay. Words fell from our lips that were different from the ways we typically love and listen to each other throughout the day. Not just different but deeper and haunting. This conversation was more of a groaning, a muttering of two and three words at a time that left me feeling more naked and exposed than I have felt since Randall died.

There's a place within me, Jonathan—a place where I feel a lot of shame—a place that I'm afraid to reveal to anybody. Even Lindsay. Because if I should open up this place to her, she may go so far inside of me I'm sure she will come running out overwhelmed and stunned by what she sees, like she's been hiking into a never-discovered cave only to find that hibernating bears have been awakened. She best get the hell out of there and run as far away from those bears—or me—as possible. I fear people getting close and knowing me like that. I must be afraid that they will leave me.

By some miracle of God, Lindsay keeps coming back and I continue to open my heart and let her in. Other times it's as if I forget she has the capacity to listen to me and accept me. At least that's my excuse for keeping conversations safe and, I'm embarrassed to say, superficial.

I run from the very thing my heart craves: intimacy.

I don't know what happened last night, sitting next to her on the sofa. We turned to hold each other as we often do, but the hug became a tender embrace, not in a sexual way, but more of a nurturing way, reassuring each of the other's love and acceptance. That we were really there for each other.

It was then that the chatter and noise in my head simply went away. Someone hit the mute button and suddenly there was only Lindsay and me in each other's arms. Then the sadness and the fears came tumbling out. "I'm afraid, Lindsay. I'm so afraid. I don't want to die." Now my tears were flowing a bit more. "I miss Randall so much. I just—I just miss him so much. I miss Lilly. I'm afraid I'm going to die, too. And soon. Everyone is leaving."

I can't remember a time in ten years when Lindsay cut me off with a sarcastic remark, so there was no reason to expect anything but her usual tender acceptance. Yet my heart was bracing for a flippant answer exhorting me to "get over it." She has never done that, but it's what I always expect when I get honest and open with people.

Maybe this is why we're so reluctant to tap those vulnerable places in ourselves. We have seldom, maybe never, had someone gently contain our feelings and fears in those naked moments. I'm sure it's all very complicated, but I know this much: when it does happen, as it did with Lindsay last night, the Spirit of God becomes almost tangible, almost physically present.

Simple conversation feels like prayer. That listening and holding and caressing another's heart—this is what our relationships were meant to look like. Not every relationship, but a few.

No wonder we feel lonely and isolated so much of the time. Nobody is ever really listening. It's too intimidating and threatening, both to the person speaking and to the person listening. It feels safer, less vulnerable, to keep the volume turned up and the chatter moving along on the surface.

As much as I long for that closeness, I find myself doing whatever it takes to avoid being present and vulnerable. Even though I know on some level that unless we're willing to be a little uncomfortable for a while, we can't cross over to that place of real connection.

Lindsay just kept holding me and reassuring me that feeling sad and afraid was okay. Some fear continues to rattle around inside of me—along with my hope and confidence. Some days the sadness returns briefly, not only missing the people who have left, but grieving over the minutes and days lost in pursuing lust or obsessing over what others think of me. This is a grief that is good and healing, even grounding me.

I am learning to welcome every emotion and not to judge them as bad or good, or me as weak or strong for having those feelings.

God is with me, and we share an awareness of all that flows in and out of my life. Whatever shows up, I know He is committed to me, His compassion and love for me are constant. I am safe with Him. Completely safe.

I don't feel as tired as I used to in my spirit. Sharing all of this with you has made me feel lighter. I feel safe with you as well.

Let me know how things go when you talk to Gina next week. It's a miracle that she's willing to talk with you. I'm pretty confident that you will be able to hear her, as I keep giving you lots of practice in listening.

I would appreciate your praying again for me—for the follow-up appointment with my doctor. He says not to worry, so I'm trying not to over-think the situation.

Also, get back to me on those Braves tickets if you can go. The Cubs will be coming to play Atlanta in a couple of weeks.

Hope to see you then,

S

Letter 15

October 30, 1988

Dear Jonathan,

I couldn't help but chuckle when you asked me to talk even more about God's mercy and grace. Surely you must know it is *you* who first shared with me in the clearest of terms how God is able to commit Himself to me fully and then love me unconditionally—because of Jesus.

Do you remember when you came to see us last year (you were a wreck!) and after dinner you pulled down a Bible from a shelf in the den? It was the Bible you gave to me and Janie for our wedding twenty-six years ago. It looks like I got custody.

The first thing you commented on was how well preserved it was. You were being kind. I think what you wanted to say is that it looks like no one has ever read it. Clumps of pages still stuck together, fresh from the box, with hardly a smudge or fingerprint anywhere except for Paul's letter to the Galatians, the Gospel of Mark, the first three chapters in Genesis and all the notations in that chapter on Christian marriage. In other words, the only pages marked in my entire Bible were from your classes I attended.

I was listening, Jonathan.

You became quiet and tearful when you realized that you were the one responsible for those words and notations. You were teaching us, Jonathan. You were leading us out of ourselves and into the Truth. You were encouraging us to think about what God was up to in our lives. As far as I am concerned, that's what you do today. Perhaps not in front of a congregation, but it's precisely what you do when you're with people, especially me. You can't help it. None of us can. What we do flows out of who we are.

I also remember your glancing up from that Book and staring off into space as if you were looking for someone to walk through the bookcase. And you started asking, almost in a whisper, "What happened? What has happened to us, Saul?"

There was so much despair and so much pain. The three of us talked past midnight.

Your haunting question is the very reason I wanted you to come immediately after your call so you could start processing what had happened. I wanted you in a quiet and safe place with people who love you. It has been my experience that I should never be left to wander around inside my head alone. It's a very scary place.

All kinds of demons and self-bashing and dark thoughts start showing up in there, especially at night when we're confused and tired. It's not safe at all. Left alone with our own thoughts, we come out bloodier and more depressed than before we went in.

Our most serious thinking won't uncover the answers we need inside ourselves. It's best we travel with someone who cares about us and isn't bogged down with an agenda of pointing out our moral failures. I don't think we can look squarely at our own darkness and defects until we feel a profound sense of acceptance settling over us, calming the relentless self-chatter of condemnation. I think it is God's loving presence among us.

Only then, from that safe place, can we actually see all the failures, the selfishness, the people we have hurt and those who have torn us to pieces. The friend who is traveling there with us does a simple thing. He listens. His listening makes room for our reality, regardless of what it is.

And when we're finally able to see it, we're less afraid and resistant because someone is looking at it with us and he hasn't bolted from the room! Very often we will find a lot of sadness and fear. And just as often, we will see the progression of our brokenness, our horrific choices and the devastation we left behind.

They are not who we are, these unimaginable things, the feelings and things we discover about ourselves. We are so much more. But we must first acknowledge and accept what we see, what we have done and what we are feeling. Eventually, I believe, we will start moving forward.

By moving forward, I hope you know that I am not assuming that well-worn cliché and very arrogant position that we must get over ourselves, forget the past, and start looking to the future. That we are essentially good people who make mistakes and all things will work out for us. That our duty is to suck it up and soldier on. This is simple-mindedness of the worst kind. Except this time it's coming not from our brothers who point out all of our specks while ignoring their own logs. This particular dancing around reality is more likely to come from the more social types who refuse to look at anything in depth, much less any of those unpleasant, disturbing feelings.

They mock any kind of soul-searching. They lack the courage to do anything that resembles a moral inventory of their lives. They are constitutionally incapable of being honest with themselves. Their comfort zone is to skim the surface of life and appear to be happy at all costs. They cannot be penetrated. They are walled off. They make me crazy, which says so much more about me than them.

I understand that they can't help it. So we must forgive them and ourselves, because none of us really knows what he is doing.

I'm wandering again. Sorry.

Actually, your questions about mercy and grace have been in the back of my mind the whole time, pushing me toward something I hope will be useful. I don't think there is a better way for us to understand any of that apart from God's initiative—from His dropping a little understanding into our lives here and there as we are able to receive it; as we let down our defenses and become willing; as we ask Him, in effect, to create a place inside of us where we can receive that unfamiliar love, mercy and acceptance.

This kind of love originates with Him, the way everything in life does. And for many, that is enough. But for me, and possibly for you, we need first to learn from a thousand different places something of God's love, and then come to truly understand and receive it as we experience that love coming from a handful of people tuned into His heart.

Let me begin by saying that mercy and grace always flow in only one direction: from His heart toward ours. Freely, abundantly, lavishly. None of it starts with us. In fact, the whole thing was worked out and secured before we were born. I also hope what I'm saying will take us past the simplistic notion that *God is love*, so we're all "in" and that is that. It's much more involved than many of us have thought about. Another good place to start might be that Jesus died and rose again *in our place*. In that ultimate sense, God has done for us what we couldn't do for ourselves. There's nothing left for us to do. There's no fine print or hidden fees. That's why it's called grace.

Our salvation is The Big Undertaking, and part of the deal is that we remain mere recipients of this grace and mercy without any bragging rights on how it all came about. Today, I don't wrestle much with being worthy. It's no secret that I am not worthy. Because of His mercy and grace, our worthiness will never become an issue.

Where I stumbled, Jonathan, was that all of this salvation talk came across to me as a kind of one-and-done package, getting my ticket to heaven punched, dodging the whole wrath of God thing.

What I got was not completely wrong. Much of it is right on the money. But much of what I got left me confused. Even today, this truncated version of the Gospel leaves me very cold, even sad. I'm now recalling those earliest explanations of the Gospel I heard coming from people who seemed more in love with the right words and correct doctrine than the God they spoke of. The same people would become tense and rigid when others didn't say "it" the way they did.

I'm discovering that the whole idea of salvation, forgiveness, redemption and justification not only includes God's forgiveness and complete acceptance of me, but also His real intentions about recovering the real me. Freeing me *in this life* of my strange, whacked-out religious beliefs, along with the delusions about my public persona, my pride and self-absorption, and my ridiculous attachment to those big and little things I'm convinced my very life depends on. All of my insane and demanding expectations of the people around me.

Jesus Christ, His necessary suffering on the cross, my forgiveness—I got that. But what I didn't get is that there is a necessary kind of suffering—the humiliation and pain, the losses and grief and confusion—that plays out in all of our lives. It's the way we grow and learn. It's the way we start letting go of our false selves and flimsy values. Suffering is not our punishment for screwing up, which a lot of religious people want us to believe. Suffering and death have always been the prelude to renewal and recovery. All of nature and the seasons themselves reveal this pattern. Human beings are the only ones who resist it.

Let me say it another way.

When Jesus said, "I am the Way," He was saying more than *This is how you get to heaven*. He was saying to us *This way—the way of deep suffering—is how we truly recover our lives and personally experience the mercy and grace of the Father*. Our suffering is where and how He reveals His mercy and grace. In the place we would never look for it. The place I would least expect to find it.

My failures, my falling apart, all the losses, the abuse I suffered as a child, the failed relationships, my addiction to alcohol and the complete collapse of my life and career. None of it was ever meant to be my undoing, but my salvation. If this is really true, I don't need to waste time thinking my failed relationships, lost jobs and public humiliation were for nothing.

None of them was wasted. They were part of the deal.

You may have noticed that I have not referred to "sin" very much in this discussion of mercy and grace. Yes, I know it's a biblical concept. I also know that, like the biblical concept of "love," it has been so misused and abused that its meaning has been reduced to nothing—except maybe as a hint at our mistakes or moral lapses from time to time that offend the cultural norm. That kind of approach actually dilutes the darkness in us all, and allows us to go on thinking generously about ourselves—that we are serious, spiritually-minded people.

For my father, sin was a kind of crime, not a desperate condition—the worst kind of spiritual cancer—that needs God's healing as well as His forgiveness. Basically, sin was anyone's failure to live up to his own lofty expectations of them; anything that threatened him, questioned his opinion or suggested that he might be wrong.

I see now that he was a very small man in his appreciation of life and people. More important, he was willfully ignorant of this deeper mercy and grace of God. They would have destroyed his paradigm for life. Letting in God's grace would have forced him to face the unavoidable conclusion that he'd had it wrong the whole time!

I refused to buy into the God of his understanding and simply said *adiós* to Jesus. I threw the proverbial baby out with the bath water.

When I was almost forty years old, I found God (actually, He found me) in the basement of the Methodist church on Nightcap Street in Chattanooga, Tennessee. Don't tempt me to speak of the irony of attending my first AA meeting on Nightcap Street. Right away I knew that God, unlike my father, had a tremendous sense of humor. That room and those meetings were the things that disarmed my bitterness toward religion and the church and uncovered my buried longing for God. One night I noticed that the crowd was much smaller than usual because the roads were icy. The thought passed through me, "There's only two or three of us gathered here tonight." I smiled and felt His presence. I've never said it quite like this before, but AA became my church.

The Twelve Steps in AA gave me the structure and guidance to live my life and take care of my needs one day at a time, all of which over many weeks, months and years created a safe and reassuring place for me to face my failures and, yes, my sins.

And so, down in that musty, smoky old basement, God's Spirit was able to peel back the layers of my shame and fears and resentment toward my father—and ultimately toward God. Through the accepting love and mercy of those men and women, I was stripped down to nothing so that I could know He loved me just as I am, not as the person I thought I was or should have been. That's how God was saving and redeeming me.

I was not able to know and experience God's love in any real way because I kept pretending to be the person I thought He and others wanted me to be. I only knew my life through how other people saw me. It is impossible for God to love and embrace our self-image. Because God is real, He can only love what is real. I'm asking God every day to help me learn simply to be the person He has always loved. Nothing more is required.

The good news is that the *real* you and me never went away. They just got hidden by all those layers of persona and self-image and the same old lies, like a gift buried in bubble wrap. Once we start getting unwrapped, safely stripped to the bare bones, emptied of all that pretense and posturing, we meet Him at last, eager as always to embrace us. The real us He has always loved.

Frankly—and this won't make much sense at first—being loved is a disarming, uncomfortable experience. It's not the scrutiny and reminders that we fall short that make us uneasy. We are very familiar with that experience. But to be embraced as we are without conditions, without shame or the dread of being judged, nothing is more unfamiliar and unsettling. That's why it will probably take me a lifetime, and a boatload of courage, to fully accept His acceptance.

Here's another way of looking at this. He let me run my life up to my complete and seemingly irreversible self-destruction. That's the front side of His grace: releasing my prodigal heart to chase after people, places and things as substitutes for Him. Then He waited for me to come to my senses. Looking back after fifteen years of staying sober, it seems to me that God was nudging my spirit, pulling me to Himself, even as he let me fall further into my own confusion and despair. Before AA and all sorts of counseling and group therapy, to which I owe my life, God was secretly jump-starting my willingness and my desire to connect with Him.

I needed major surgery. For me this surgery came in the form of hitting bottom—more like falling through the bottom—then finding myself in the presence of other men with the same disease and despair. A bunch of love cripples, suffering with the same doubts and fears.

I needed not only some super kind of love, but a tender touch—a human touch. Real people showing mercy and compassion to me, giving me a sense that healing was possible. The hope that not drinking and recovering my life could actually happen.

Hope came from and through those men who did for me what no parent, lover, friend, teacher or minister had ever done. They listened to me. They loved me. Never judging me. Without the faintest hint of disgust. And, as they shared with me their own stories, hope seeped back into my heart a little bit every day.

So when you ask me to give you a better understanding of God's mercy and grace, I do what I know. I tell my story. I have no other reference point. Otherwise, it's purely theoretical.

God's mercy and compassion, His unconditional acceptance of me—none of it became real to me until I got honest and told my story to a handful of recovering addicts. This is the way it works, Jonathan. If we tell our stories over and over, if we keep sharing our trails of deceit and confusion and despair and powerlessness, if we keep doing that with the people who accept us in spite of what they might hear, we *will* start telling the truth.

We're skeptical at first. Not too trusting. Always testing the waters. Every experience from the past has wired us to believe a lie: *Tell the truth and you're screwed.*

We wrap ourselves in what someone described as "silky layers of illusion" that hold us securely in a false reality. The layers come off slowly. Every time we tell our story another layer comes off, then another. We go deeper, get more real, bringing our secrets into the light. And yet the people we've been talking to are still there—knowingly, warmly taking in every word. They are moved by neither the grossness of our acts or the sincerity of our confession. We are telling and they are hearing our story. And all of us are being healed.

When we tell our stories to others, it brings everything out into the open, and all the resentment and guilt and fear loosen their grip on our lives. So we keep coming back and telling our story hundreds, eventually thousands of times. The honesty and vulnerability begin to feel normal. For the first time in our lives, we feel safe. We are stepping out of the shadows and learning a new way to live.

The goal is not to reach an imaginary place of perfect honesty. The goal is to tell our story as honestly as we know how.

Eventually, we are telling the truth and seeing the truth. That very human impulse to cover and defend ourselves, to cast the best light on our behavior, will never completely leave us. But as long as we keep telling our stories, the compulsion gets weaker. I don't understand all that I know. I just know that this is how it has worked for me.

There's another facet to this telling of our stories. We become more vulnerable, and, strangely, more compassionate, because we start hearing our story in the stories of others. We're not so defensive. We don't feel as critical and judgmental. The urgent need to be right about everything begins to fade.

But here's the biggest surprise. In telling my story again and again, I'm discovering that my story never was just about me. When all the ups and downs, failures and successes, humiliations and adulations are added up, what we discover is that our stories have been about Someone else—usually behind the scenes, hidden from our awareness, doing for us what we couldn't and often wouldn't do for ourselves. If I'm right, it means that my story fits into a larger story, one that God has been writing all along. It feels weird even talking this way. But I think it's true.

Jonathan, I'm guessing that He's not only writing a good story for us, but He's been pursuing us the whole time with that untiring mercy we've hungered for since the day we were born. For that reason I now see that every step of the way, every time I got crazy with a woman or staggered through my front door drunk out of my mind, every piece of my broken and wounded life not only came at a high price, but was absolutely necessary.

We will continue this conversation for many days to come. We'll have plenty of time when you drive down for Thanksgiving. This will be our first weekend of feasting on college football in a long time. I want you to call me as soon as you hear from Gina, if you feel so inclined. I'll understand if you need some time first to process everything she says.

One more thing. I have a letter here from Maureen saying that JJ is not well. God knows he has lived twenty years longer than anyone expected. It's his lungs. I think it would be okay to tell Gina when she calls.

Lindsay and I love you. I thank God every day that you're back in my life.

See you soon,

S

Letter 16

January 7, 1989

Dear Jonathan,

The news about Jess has caught me completely off guard. It seemed so sudden and unexpected. Lindsay and I will come down this weekend.

Smoking takes a toll. Good Lord, I wonder if that's what's going to get me eventually. All those Camels and Lucky Strikes I smoked for thirty-plus years. Which reminds me, Lindsay wanted me to mention that the doctor has given me a clean bill of health. They want to see me in a year. Thank you for praying for my sanity, as well as the doctor's report.

Your response to the news has been amazing. That's not surprising because I know how much you love your father. I sense your gratitude for being able to give him the care he will need.

In a day, an instant, our lives can be shattered or reversed beyond recognition. My mind goes back to the night you called in your moment of terrible darkness and desperation. I'll never understand what prompted you to think of me and my letters then. It was a day of infamy for you, but a day of restored hope for me. It is so humbling, and such a blessed thing, to realize that Lindsay and I became the first stop on your journey back to Him.

Rummaging through these things reminds me of the limitations of our understanding. That what we see as a tragedy today may in fact be the bridge to the most wonderful period of our lives. That it's important not to get caught up in labeling everything that happens as good or bad. We're not to judge—neither people and their motivations nor the ebb and flow of our daily lives. A judgment about anything is ultimately a judgment about Him.

Our first response in any situation should rightly be acceptance, to surrender to what has happened and in faith accept it as coming from His hand. I keep this reminder from the AA Big Book on my desk: "Nothing, absolutely nothing happens in God's world by mistake."

The "goodness" or "badness" that grips us is diminished by letting in the possibility that in *all* things He is good, brimming over with that grace and mercy we talked about. Then the peaks and valleys of our human experience somehow become shorter and shallower as our capacity to accept life on life's terms grows more solid and consistent.

Instead of accepting life on "life's terms," I suppose it's more correct to say "God's terms." But that sounds way too harsh for me, like He's going to dump whatever He chooses into our pathetic little lives and we best get used to it! I think it's more of a realization that His purpose is to remove everything that hinders us from depending on and loving Him—even our cherished ideas and notions about Him. It was Lewis who put that thought into me years ago when he said in class one day, "I want God, not my idea of God."

I'm sounding a bit pious here. (How I detest that in others!) My hope is that by reminding myself about His goodness, something in me will come to truly let it and Him in. Something I can feel inside, you know, not just theories and lofty words.

But you know me, Jonathan. I am quick to judge people and circumstances. I find myself making everything an enemy. So I react and let worry grind away at me. I have learned to accept myself this way, grossly imperfect with a knee-jerk reaction to insult or infringement. Such acceptance is a start. I'm not going to make it all the way to perfection, which I believe is not only impossible but highly overrated. We're not perfect. We're not complete. And we never will be. In fact, perfection was never the plan. The plan has always been to go out and live boldly with all of our imperfections. That's what makes certain people attractive—not that they have it all together, but that they're so incredibly comfortable not having it all together.

Our lives get so complicated, it seems. But are they really? Or do they just feel jumbled when we're trying to control everything? I remember when you first started feeling a bit lighter, when hope started returning—hope in your spirit after the overwhelming personal loss and destruction from your affair, Gina's leaving, losing your position at church—and the list goes on. Our lives have been parallel in so many ways, Jonathan. We both experienced breakdowns, fear and hopelessness and all those wonderful things that we struggle to avoid but eventually find on our doorstep.

I often feel like a victim. Passive, never taking the initiative, able to respond only to what's coming at me. It's called survival. That's the most prevalent approach I have taken—just surviving.

We don't start out that way. In the beginning we're all engaging and happy and charging forward, innocent children at least for a while. But then our small, separate lives get complicated. Disappointments and losses pile up. Fear kicks in at every turn and so much is being thrown at us that all we can do is react. Hang on. Survive.

I got a haircut yesterday and the teenage girl a chair over was shown a gray hair popping through her perfectly highlighted mane. She let out one of those teenager "I'm so pissed" groans. "Oh m'god, I can't handle this!" Poor girl. I saw myself in her in that moment. Before, I would have mumbled something under my breath like, "For God's sake girl, get a life." Not now.

Each of us feels the weight of our problems in a very individual way. It feels overwhelming no matter what the age or how grave (or frivolous) the problem. For that fifteen-year-old, it was discovering a gray hair. Horror! At nineteen it will be not getting a bid from the "right" sorority. When she's forty-one, it will be discovering a lump in her breast. The response will be consistent: "Oh m'god, I can't handle this!"

Scott Peck was right when he wrote in *The Road Less Traveled*, "Life is difficult." He wasn't inferring that we're all a bunch of victims, although we think we are, or that life just happens to us and we're stuck with it.

Real life for me—which means not seeing myself or living as a victim—began when I realized that what makes life difficult is not the gray hair or social ostracism or dreading a positive biopsy. What puts me at odds with life is my own broken capacity to respond openly and vulnerably to whatever flows into my life.

I resist and resist and resist like a rock in a river. This resistance to life, the struggle to make life work on our own terms, seems to start early and last until the day we die. Because I make life acutely personal and all about me, life is horrifically difficult and demanding and overwhelming. At times I hate it. And then I say, "Oh m'god, I can't handle this!" Being stressed out feels normal. But that, I am learning, was never the plan.

God often gives us what we want, but not always. Whatever happens, however, we can be confident that He is bringing or letting into our lives the stuff we need. For you, it seems, it's this slice of time with your father you never had after your mother died. Usually it's something external that makes us slow down and realize that a much-needed season of healing has arrived. The challenge is to accept it as a gift and stay in it. We're always in such a damn hurry.

I don't think we know what we have been longing for until years later when, in some serendipitous moment, the chance for a mere ten minutes of unrushed conversation with a friend or, in your case, with your father, plops in our lap and our body is flooded with never-before-experienced peace and satisfaction.

This, we declare, is what we've wanted all along! Not the toys, just our father's opening himself to us and being present. As we feel everything being stripped away, we're invited to show up with whatever is left—just ourselves. In that instant, we realize that had always been enough. Nothing more is required.

Jess is looking at death, and you are lost. This lostness is simply a "not knowing" what to do or how to think about things. That's not always a bad thing; it just feels terrible and irreversible. My question is, how can we allow this sense of being lost and adrift to become a place of acceptance and deep satisfaction?

We have both been brought to places where we're forced to slow down and focus. Here's Jess, getting sicker every day. Your father is dying. And here you are in a shattered marriage and feeling humiliated. Like many wandering sons, you got to go back to your father. And, as always, he takes you in one more time.

If Jess leaves one mark on our lives it will be that certain people will always be there for us no matter what. Like JJ, he has always been planting in us that seed of hope: could God really be like this, graciously waiting and always eager for us to come to Him? Always there for us? I'm beginning to think so.

I understand, Jonathan. I was forced to slow down and be with my dad. God knew I needed that time, and time was running out. I had missed my father all my life. I feared him at every level. I only knew him as that raging, abusive religious fanatic, and I hated him. The version of my father that I heard from others didn't match what I saw growing up.

It's so confusing; very weird. I never knew he was a good guy to more than a few people. That he was more than his failures and abusive behavior at home. Yet to them he had a heart, and on some level, I must now conclude, he truly loved God and loved people, including me in some twisted sort of way.

He was a very wounded soul. His wounds festered into a raging bitterness and emotional violence toward all of his children. He connected with us only at those wounded, unhealed places. Never heart to heart.

He's a perfect caricature of all of us. We have these parts that are so generous and good and loving, and then we see the rage or fear or resentments lash out at others—almost coming out of us sideways—and we say, "What was that all about? Where did that darkness come from?"

Father, forgive us, for we truly don't know what we are doing. And we certainly don't know what we're doing to others, especially the ones we try to love.

I guess it's safe to assume that God loved my dad and understood the depths of his pain, his sin, and found some place in him where He could make the assertion, "You belong to me." This did not overcome my dad's defects of character, it didn't bring the measure of healing in his life that I've been blessed with, but eventually it was enough.

At the very end, that light of love and the hope that had remained buried in him his entire life emerged briefly, and we had a very short but tender season of connecting heart to heart.

These deeper glimpses of grace and mercy help me know that I am, if nothing else, a forgiven man. And because of that forgiveness, I have been given the freedom to take my hands from my father's throat and release him from my entrenched bitterness and resentments. I wanted him dead most of my life. But once I saw that we were both broken men and desperate for love, the only response can be, "Lord, have mercy on me."

I know you feel the same way, Jonathan. It's obvious that something deep and profound is unfolding in your life. We are both encouraged hearing from Gina. She called me asking about Jess the same day she spoke with you. I don't think I'm violating her confidentiality by saying she asked about you as well. Quite tenderly, I might add.

This is a good thing. Unlike me, I know you will not read too much into her overture and start making plans for a second honeymoon. What I'm trying to say is that she felt safe, it seems, and willing to see where things might go for the two of you.

So while we grieve about your dad, we have much to be grateful for.

We were built to handle all of this, weren't we? All the stuff about weeping with those who are broken hearted, and being excited for those who are having a good day.

Lindsay and I will drive down Friday after classes and take the two of you to dinner. Tell Jess as often as possible how much we love him and that we are praying that God would heal him.

Love from us both,

S

Letter 17

April 9, 1989

Dear Jonathan,

I'm glad you didn't know what was going on. When I realized that there was not a police escort to Arlington, I panicked. I found a phone in one of the offices down the hall and started making calls.

For me, it was something of a miracle. But it started out as one of the most ridiculous things I've ever seen—that the Cobb County Police would not cross the Chattahoochee and take us into Fulton County to Arlington Cemetery. I stopped fooling around with them and called the Atlanta Police downtown.

They put me on hold, of course, and passed me around to a half-dozen pencil pushers. At last somebody with authority picked up the phone, a Captain Jensen, but I couldn't make out a word he was saying. His mouth was full of marbles.

He probably had no idea what I was talking about either. I just kept yelling like a Pentecostal preacher over the racket in the police station. "A funeral! Pine Ridge! We need the police! To Sandy Springs!"

Finally he blurted out an intelligent question. "Son, whose funeral are you talking about?"

"Jess Goodson. Jesse S. Goodson, Pine Ridge, Georgia," I shouted back. "We're at the Little River Church on Hills Ferry Road."

Then the most amazing thing happened. In a calm and deliberate voice, Captain Jensen asked, "Is that the Jess Goodson who owns the hardware stores?

"Yes, that's him."

"Son, I've known Jess Goodson for forty years! Hell of a man!" He sounded genuinely happy at the memory. "Always talking about his pretty wife. He had a son, didn't he? Played football. I'll be damned! Who am I talking to?"

"My name is Saul Bates. I'm Mr. Goodson's brother-in-law."

"Mr. Bates, don't worry about a thing. I'll have your escort at the church in ten minutes. Please tell Mrs. Goodson we're real sorry."

Ten minutes later, like magic, two motorcycles roared up to the front of the Little River Church while we were singing "How Great Thou Art." Jess made that happen.

After talking to the captain, I slumped over the desk in that little office for several more minutes. It wasn't that I was overcome with grief, it was more like Someone sat me down for a very brief but focused moment to let me take it all in. To understand what I had just experienced in this random conversation with a man I had never met and will never see or speak to again.

In that moment, Jonathan, I saw things as they are. How our lives intersect the lives of others in the most mundane and un-heroic ways. I saw the way Jess loved Lilly and you and everything about his life before she died. I could see him in my mind's eye arriving at his hardware store at 6:30 in the morning ready to meet the day. I remembered how he would cup his hot coffee in both hands while standing on the sidewalk, watching the dawn's light streaking across the Atlanta skyline.

He would stand there alone with his thoughts until a twenty-year-old cop would pull up in a patrol car, roll down his window and holler, "Mornin'

Jess." And your dad would answer, "Arrested anybody yet?"

Jensen would park his car and the two of them would stand on the sidewalk and drink coffee and talk—not about arresting criminals or selling tools and fertilizer but about their families and their kids.

I know that until recently it would have been hard to imagine your dad's engaging in an in-depth conversation with anyone. I understand that changed for you and him over the last three months. His terminal illness and your uncertain future eventually merged into the gift of intimate time between you and your dad. Jess could say what needed to be said in a sentence and it would stay with you for a long, long time. His was a deep, uncomplicated wisdom that pulled people toward him, then drew them back again and again because they wanted more of what he had, more of who he was.

The people who knew and loved your father, my brother, didn't need to dissect what they were experiencing. They just felt safe and accepted. They felt heard. Like their lives really mattered. If I could ask them what drew them to Jess—to define that magnet—they would say it was his heart.

We can track to the day when something shifted in Jess. When Lilly died, something else died in Jess. Although he was still the same gracious man, his balance and poise were gone. His drive and focus disappeared and he seemed more on the defensive, even nervous.

He showed up, remained faithful and true as ever, but the joy had left him.

We can't fake joy, Jonathan. Exuberance and enthusiasm can be mimicked for a while out of habit, performing for others perhaps. But not that unmistakable Mark of Life. We either have it or we don't. It takes a huge amount of personal awareness to admit there is a void. Yet before we can hope to recover any amount of joy, we must admit that we don't have it. That's not defeat, that's our honest, broken heart longing for God to heal us.

It is a rare thing in itself to admit something isn't quite right with our lives. Most of us just act angry or upset, looking for some person or situation to blame for things being out of sorts. The first step for me is to admit my powerlessness, the absence of joy, the real state of things—and stay in that place for a while, observing the hurts and longings of my heart. If I can just be patient and wait and be quiet, the answers will come.

Yet even with all the sadness and loss, that wonderful transparency and gift for "telling it like it is" never deserted your father. Few memories are burned into my brain as deeply as the moment during Helen's funeral when he and I were standing side by side looking at her body in the casket. He looked at her, then over at me, then back down, and shook his head ever so slightly as the hint of a smile played across his face.

"Saul, she was mean as cat shit."

That says a lot—about the both of them.

After Lilly died Jess was observant and perceptive, but behind the eyes empty and lifeless. Like the eyes of a red snapper in the freezer.

There was an unmistakable emptiness to my life for the longest time, until some things set all that healing into motion.

The obvious one people point to is the day Lindsay and I met. Her love and transparency are so constant and nurturing, so much a part of me now that I actually don't think about them very much. Not that I take her for granted, it's just that there's no need to question or worry about her being with me. She is above all else my lover and my wife, my best friend, but on another level she has created a peaceful harbor for me where my life has been gently re-parented.

When I became more transparent and honest about my resentments and sadness, parts of me that had been dead and ignored for years came alive. I noticed trees changing their colors, children laughing and playing together, and just how blue the sky really is. For the first time in my life, I could hear people talk about

God's love without acting like my typical cynical self. I had been shut down to everything, Jonathan. Nothing could get in. Not even His love.

Another factor in my healing probably came when I stopped running from my past and slowed down enough to realize that I am truly a product of my childhood. I now know that all the experiences with the people who cared for me (or were at least supposed to care for me) got permanently tucked away in my subconscious. The way they looked at me when they were happy or sad, they way they spoke to me when they were angry or loving or disappointed, the smells and the times of day—that whole drama is preserved forever in my heart. Their fingerprints are all over me to this day. Those people still live in my head as a forceful advisory committee, shaping the way I see and understand and feel about myself and my wildly imperfect world.

If my journey had stopped there—just seeing how everything got screwed up—I would have remained a helpless child, a complete victim, shaking my fist and blaming everyone for my failures, heartaches and lost opportunities. Still trapped in that smaller, pain-filled reality.

Learning how to be honest opened my heart and let me know that today my choices belong to me alone. I am not only the product of my childhood, but also of the choices I made and the meanings I gave to those events and experiences. Yes people hurt me; yes I made poor choices because as a child I couldn't know any better. But today, it's my decision whether to be a victim or take full responsibility for the choices I am making and the person I am becoming.

By becoming aware of all that went on in my childhood—particularly with the people who made the biggest impact, like my dad and Randall, and especially Lilly—I can re-frame and assign new meanings to those experiences and events with a deeper understanding and, most especially, with greater compassion toward that little boy and those wounded adults who touched his life. I can acknowledge again that nothing, absolutely nothing, happens in God's world by mistake.

No mistakes. Now, that's a comforting thought. Nonetheless, I must confess that Lindsay and I are pretty anxious about seeing both you and Gina this weekend. It will be an awkward but necessary first step. I am cautiously hopeful of seeing you two back together someday.

Praying for all,

L

Letter 18

May 17, 1989

Dear Jonathan,

The walk we took down by the creek during our last visit has left me with more questions than answers. I'm not sure what you were after, but you got me wondering where my life would have gone had my mother not died. The only possible scraps of memories would be from my time in her womb, which remain hidden from me for now.

Lilly was a young teenager when our mother died while giving birth to me. My God, Jonathan, as I write these words, I am realizing for the first time that Lilly was only fourteen when her mother died—just like you. We must talk about that soon.

From Lilly mostly I learned that our mother had a wonderful smile and a reputation for teasing people in a good-humored sort of way. That she always wore a fragrance called White Shoulders. I know the scent well, and I find myself missing her when I pass a woman wearing it. I also learned much later from Lilly that our father usually didn't get her jokes and pranks. He would put her down for being silly or sacrilegious, and, of course, quote the appropriate Scripture to underscore his righteous indignation. She ignored him most of the time—a wonderful trait she passed on to me.

Your mother faithfully showed to me pictures of my mother until I was about six or seven years old, when she and Jess fell in love and got married. After that, she kept a few pictures of Mom in wooden frames on the bookcases in her living room. If she saw me staring at one, she would stop whatever she was doing to tell me the special story behind that particular picture. Eventually I could just glance at any photograph while walking through the house and instantly recall the people and the stories surrounding that particular scene. Some of the best memories I have of my family, I'm sad to say, are of things that occurred before I was born.

One stands out, and it comes from a picture taken about a week before I was born—and my mother died—Saturday, April 10, 1937. I'm not sure who took the picture, perhaps my father, because he is not in this family portrait. Lilly and Randall are standing just behind Mother, who is turned slightly to her right, facing Lilly, putting her full-term pregnancy on display.

Lilly is standing to her right in the photo, only two inches shorter than her mother. Her right hand is on top of her mother's two hands resting on her big belly. Randall, six feet tall and now driving, reaches around the expectant mother with his left hand on the very top of his mother's and sister's. I suppose this "laying on of hands" was their way of acknowledging me as a very real part of the family. This is something Lilly tried to help me understand—that I belonged to these people and that they loved me.

All three in the picture are looking at me, that is, the bulge under my mother's navy blue smock, and wearing big smiles. Randall is laughing because our mother is kidding around and having a conversation with me as if I am responding to her in complete sentences, saying things like, "Boy, it sure is dark in here! Did ya'll forget to pay the light bill?" Everyone seems enthusiastic about my arrival.

I exhausted Lilly asking her repeatedly to tell me the story behind this particular shot. Frustrated one day, she sternly asked me (I am told) if

I possibly knew another word besides "again." In self-defense, she developed a long and a short version of the narrative. She frequently tried to slip me the *Cliff's Notes* version, but I would moan and complain until she relented and promised to wade through every detail one more time.

It was her own fault, because she told the story with so much passion and imagination and color, and, most importantly, she made the story all about me.

Your mother and father unexpectedly walked into my dorm room one night when I was a freshman at Tech. I had not seen them in almost a month. The blinds were pulled tight and the room was pitch black. I was out cold, probably hung-over, but she was able to rouse me from a deep sleep by blurting out, "Boy, it sure is dark in here! Did ya'll forget to pay the light bill?"

That was the short version. I sat up in bed and threw my pillow at her.

I couldn't get enough; it was my first addiction. Her voice comforted me, even though I didn't know I needed comforting. Her stories anchored my spirit and re-assured me that I belonged in this world even without a mother and, in some ways, without a father. I had no vocabulary for my feelings. I can only guess that I was an insecure child, probably very anxious.

Lilly was my lifeline. Something every child needs. I know that my dependency on my sister was healthy and normal. But out of those repeated experiences I got wired a certain way, and cultivated a dependency on anything that would help me achieve in fantasy what I couldn't find in reality.

At some point, I learned that I could drink— not to feel good, but to help me not feel bad. I found that I could live with almost any situation when I had something or someone to help medicate my disappointments and fears. I barely had any understanding of this until I had been sober for three or four years. I guess you could say I became an adult when I was nearly fifty years old, intentionally surrendering at long last my ways of coping with life that I had learned as a child. It was time for me to grow up.

I used to rant at another picture. Rage might be better. On the center shelf just to the right of the mantle, that little black and white of my parents on the day they became engaged. She is nineteen. He is twenty-five. She is smiling and wearing a wide-brim straw hat. He is wearing a skinny black tie and a white short-sleeved shirt, squeezing a twenty-pound Bible under his left arm. That should have tipped off somebody.

They've known each other for three weeks and my father, legend has it, believed that God told him they should be married as soon as possible. Don't ever ask me what I think of people who are certain that God has spoken to them.

My mother doesn't know it, but she has already lived half her life.

But I know it. That's when I want to crawl into the picture, pull her aside and say, "You don't have to do this, Katherine! Not now! You can wait!"

And my mother says to me, "I know, Saul. I'm having some doubts. But he's a good man, and he does love God so."

In all the "talks" we've had over the years, not once have I heard her say to me, "I love him."

Of course this is ridiculous. I know what you're thinking, and you're right. Had my mother not made this colossal mistake there never would have been a Saul or a Lilly Bates. This means that Jess Goodson would have married Charlene Fleming from Cherokee High School because he would have never been swept off his feet by your gorgeous mother. Furthermore, apart from this nineteen-year-old girl's reckless decision to marry the man who became my father I would never have known you. The rest is more than obvious.

So you see, Jonathan, even though I actually never knew this person, what I do know is that through the choices she made, my mother keeps finding ways to touch me every day of my life.

I'm not sure why, but somehow I am comforted by all of this. The question is really not, "What would my life be like if my mother had not died?" No, it's more like, "In what ways has my life been affected because

Katherine Bates *was* my mother, that she *did* live?"

In answering that question, I can understand—with so much gratitude and wonder—that she has always been a part of my life; that she has been nurturing and guiding me in ways, though obscure to me, that are no less real than the tangible and life-altering ways Lilly and you and Lindsay have affected me.

You will be glad to hear that I think God is behind all of this. He must be. Otherwise how can any of us feel hopeful? It's much more flattering to believe that we are guided by a mature and seasoned perspective molded through our careful study and understanding of Scripture, or the humble seeking of God's wisdom through diligent prayer and meditation. I suppose it actually happens that way sometimes. But just look at our lives, and the results of our best and most sincere intentions. On the surface, the whole thing appears to be nothing more than a crapshoot.

The paths we actually take and all the decisions we make, including my mother's, are more often than not based upon our desperate need for approval, raging hormones, the cold pizza we ate for breakfast, or just plain fear. Ministers, in my opinion, want us to believe that God is in the business of revealing a polished, perfect will for us to simply follow and obey. If we miss it, we're the only ones to blame. After we wander from The Path, the best any of us can do is pursue a kind of second tier, watered-down version of God's best for what's left of our misguided lives.

When I read the Scriptures today, I come across people like me whose lives are piled high with horrific choices, poor judgment and mindless behavior. Just name one person, other than Jesus, who seemed to get it right even occasionally.

In the last few years I have come to believe that the Bible is true, not because of airtight, indisputable arguments for inerrancy, but because it tells the truth, revealing even its heroes as flawed, struggling mortals. This must be the Spirit of God speaking through these writers because, left to themselves, they would be more like us, spinning the facts to protect and enhance our reputations.

From where does this feeling of hope spring? I'm not really sure, except that I sense it in myself and I see it in you, Jonathan. We've created monstrous calamities from the choices we have made. We didn't plan our lives that way, but we've gone down those roads that should have led, for all counts, to a miserable end.

Then Something intervened.

And what about all the broken people in the Bible? Their joy and passion seem boundless—a radically different disposition from those who for some strange reason persist in judging the weaknesses of others, while implying that they seldom if ever stray from The Path. There is no joy in them, only smug satisfaction. I think they're faking it, pretending to have it all together and persuading no one but themselves.

This deeper kind of joy, hope and comfort seems to rest only on those who have embraced and owned the messes they've made and the hurt and pain they've brought upon other lives. There's no shrinking back from admitting their responsibility and guilt.

But they also recognize that something else is going on, mysteriously rearranging all of these broken pieces and gently healing wounded and shattered lives. At some point they seem both hopeful and relieved, like I felt after admitting my own powerlessness over alcohol and the hundreds of failed attempts to manage my own life.

Yes, there is great relief and a sense of forgiveness, which is always followed by gratitude. And there's something else. I can't quite describe the thing—it feels a bit awkward for me—but I am sure that worship and praise (of God) come very close to describing it. These things—the hope, the gratitude, even the praise—are showing up more and more in my life. No one is more surprised than I am.

I am eager to put a name on whatever this is that has begun redeeming and reclaiming the messes we have made and the heartaches we have caused others. You have my permission, Jonathan, to straighten out my theology later, but I'm going to take a shot and call this thing *mercy*, because it has brought me so much healing, such a deep sense of acceptance, and some expectation about being made whole again. In my own experience, mercy is so undeserved, so unexpected and so lavish. It's so devoid of judgment, shame and isolation, so foreign to my experience—except for the glimpses I received from you and Lilly and, of course, JJ. It's unmanageable. I cannot control it. I can only receive it. Out of this experience with mercy (I think this is the Source) flow my joy and my hope and, I think, the longing to know more.

I want to hear everything about your moving back to Nashville and the prospects of your going with Gina to see Jeremy McNair. He's an unbelievable therapist. Lindsay and I would not be where we are today without his direction and wisdom.

I wasn't always so fond of this man. He may not be a fit for the two of you, but do give him some time. Over the last twenty years, I've run through several therapists and counselors. One of them actually fired me, threw me out of his office. But Jeremy McNair is unique, so gifted and special. He knows that I love him dearly and owe my life to him.

Lindsay and I will continue to pray for you—for both of you.

Love,

L

Letter 19

August 18, 1989

Dear Jonathan,

I know you've been incredibly busy settling your father's affairs. And as if all that weren't enough, you've got the situation with Gina—the shock, confusion and despair of her pulling away from the counseling. I can't imagine how that must feel.

Gina's decision took me by surprise. Maybe I was being a bit naïve, but in our last conversation she sounded so open and hopeful. Apparently she is not ready to go forward with you and Jeremy. She doesn't want to meet, doesn't want to talk, doesn't want to dig in and look at things.

Though that's disappointing, I don't think it's necessarily over between the two of you. Don't despair. Not yet, anyway. Let the whole situation breathe for a while. That initial looking inside ourselves with someone like Jeremy can be a harrowing experience. It's not unusual for us to want to run as far and as fast as we can when we're invited to do some deeper soul work—"shadow work" some people call it.

I know you had very high expectations going into those sessions. Hearing the news knocks the wind out of you. Are you sure she's retaining an attorney? If so, that's not a good sign, but neither is it hopeless. She can still choose to become invested in rebuilding your relationship, but she has to move at her own pace.

Having all that on your plate is more than enough. Please don't feel bad about not being able to help Maureen and me move JJ into his new apartment. It wasn't all that difficult. I can tell you he's definitely primed and ready for your first visit. You already know the place well. Cherokee Woods. It's the same assisted living facility in Canton where your grandfather lived his last two years.

It took Maureen and me less than thirty minutes to get JJ settled. He has a simple one-bedroom apartment, which we had looking like home in no time. We set up his furniture, hauled in his big black trunk, arranged three or four small boxes of his pictures, albums and various keepsakes, and we were done. That's all he has in the world, everything he needs to be content.

He asked me especially to bring one of his prized possessions, a plastic model of the *USS Missouri*, the World War II battleship you put together and gave to him when you were in the fifth grade. It still looks great. *Big Mo* now sits proudly on the top shelf, right next to a black and white photo of you, me, JJ and Buck's mother at the Pine Ridge football banquet in 1961. Mercy, how the memories came flooding back.

We all knew this time for him had to come, Jonathan. JJ must stay connected to an oxygen tank all the time—he pulls it along behind him like a tiny golf cart—and he's way too big for Maureen to bathe and shave and dress every day like she's been doing forever. I can't believe Maureen is almost eighty years old. This move will mark the first time in nearly fifty years that she will not be JJ's primary caregiver. She's had that job every single day, seven days a week for her entire adult life.

Jonathan, I want to prepare you for something you probably won't be expecting when you go to see him. Something that feels very timely considering all that you're dealing with right now. On JJ's mirror is a fairly large picture of *you*, taped in the upper left hand corner. It's the only picture on the mirror, and it's actually the first thing you notice when you walk into the room. The picture was taken when you were in high school at Pine Ridge.

Maureen left after we had dinner so it was just the two of us, me sitting on the love seat and JJ in his recliner. My curiosity was getting the best of me, so I started asking some questions.

"JJ, what's the story behind that picture of Jonathan? It's a great picture. Is there a reason why you put it up there on your mirror?"

Well, his face absolutely lights up the room, and I can feel him searching for just the right words to give me an answer. His breathing is very labored, and when he talks now he's gasping between each word like a nervous groom repeating his marriage vows, panting and punching out the words one at a time as the minister slowly recites them. Listening to him talk is incredibly tedious, but in some mysterious way, very powerful, because he makes me pay attention to everything going on.

He's drooling and he's breathing hard as he gets out one syllable, then the next, and the next.

I...pway...fuh...Ja...nu...thun...evie...day.

That...he...luv...gee...zus...like...me.

As my eyes watered up, I tried slowly repeating JJ's own words back to him, hoping to keep my emotions in check.

"You pray for Jonathan every day?" He nods "yes," pleased that I understood him, and starts pushing out that second cluster of words, "So he will love Jesus—like me."

Do you see what he was saying? Your picture on the mirror has been *the* reminder to pray for you Jonathan, to pray for you every day—*that you will love Jesus the way he loves Jesus*.

I just sat in silent amazement. Then I started crying softly. I'm not sure why. The tears just came. Without seeing your face or hearing your voice, I know that when you read this letter you will be feeling what I felt sitting in that room.

I too have prayed for you, Jonathan. God knows how I have prayed for you over the years. But I was never certain that I was praying for the right things. I didn't understand much of what praying was supposed to do, if anything. I figured God knew about your situation, so my prayers always sounded like I was giving him a "to do" list, as if He needed me to keep Him well-informed about what was best for you. It felt kind of silly at times. I guess I just talked to God and asked Him to help you, to protect you and bless you and, selfishly I suppose, bring us back together some day.

But JJ prays in a different way. Here's a handicapped child who has grown into a remarkable, yet very odd man. A man who cannot bathe or dress himself, a fully grown man who cannot read, who can barely put three words together, who frequently soils himself and constantly drools down the front of his shirt. He will never hold a job or play a sport or write a check or own a house. He will never drive a car or vote or get married or raise a family. By every standard that our world demands of us and we demand of each other, JJ is a loser, a misfit, a retard or worse.

There have been some rare and fleeting moments in my life when a curtain is pulled back, like on a stage, and I discover that the stuff I call reality, the world I live in, actually lies inside a greater world and a more real reality. There is a more rock-bottom reality. Though I couldn't put a name on the situation when those moments passed before or through me, I knew somehow that this greater, rock-bottom reality belonged to God.

Every day JJ speaks your name to God and connects you, Jonathan, to the goodness and grace filling that Larger Reality, the reality he lives in all day long.

JJ's only ambition is to love Jesus and see that we love Him, too. That's the reality he lives in. This unfiltered life of prayer brings him into the presence of God for one thing: to help us love Jesus; to lead us to a passionate, reckless devotion to the God Who loves us. There's a remarkable wisdom in that little-boy brain frozen inside a man's body. Somehow it seems to know and to offer the only thing any of us really needs.

Every time I'm with JJ I am reminded that where he is spiritually is where I belong as well. I spend such a big portion of my life fretting over things and people because my life is lived in that smaller world: the world where I pay my bills, teach English classes, coach baseball, travel with my wife, talk to you and go to AA meetings. No wonder it all feels very empty sometimes. Yet living out of that reality is all that most of us ever know about. And it cannot sustain us.

This smaller reality that we cobble together isn't an evil thing, an immoral or sinful or bad thing. I just forget that it's not the *only* thing. Most of the anguish in my life comes from this incurable forgetting that there is a larger, more real reality. It's a kind of spiritual amnesia.

I not only forget, I coast a lot. I drift. It's not automatic for me to live from this wider perspective. Something usually has to come along that shatters my little world: a disappointment, a humiliation, one of those necessary losses I try to avoid at all cost. Something that will wake me up, bring me to my knees and remind me that my reality is not the ultimate reality and doesn't have the last word on anything. This, I am learning, is another way God unveils His mercy to us and draws us back to Himself.

JJ has a real advantage over you and me, Jonathan. The container that holds his life is so thin and fragile, he *must* live out of the center, out of that deeper, rock-bottom reality. He's less encumbered than we are by all of the self-regulating and self-protecting filters that check and measure our responses to life.

By contrast, our actions are so filtered and measured that they're often dead wrong. They compel us to compare ourselves to others, inform us if we are worthy, let us know if we have done enough. Our problem is that we have a choice. We get hard-wired with these sabotaging beliefs and flatter ourselves that we've figured things out. These personal filters keep us tethered to our smaller reality. They keep us locked in our tit-for-tat, black and white, merit-badge-wearing world where we must be always performing, always competing, always on the defensive, always having to be right.

This smaller reality that we defend so fiercely usually has little or no room for mercy and grace. It dictates who can and can't be forgiven, who gets our wrath or who gets our acceptance, who's "in" and who's "out." In the Larger Reality, the reality that belongs to God, we're always surprised to see how all of that plays out, who gets forgiven and healed and restored. In this Larger Reality, everything and everyone can be forgiven and redeemed. Our reality stretches only as far as we can see. God's reality reaches as far as He can see.

I've come to the conclusion that some of us have a much harder time overcoming the limited beliefs we acquired growing up; a harder time letting go of all the personal images, roles and our pretentious false selves. We can't let go because we have so much invested in them.

Then there are the precious people like JJ living on the margin: the poor, the destitute and the desperate; the folks in jail or rehab centers; the helpless and the handicapped; the moral failures and spiritual outcasts. The crowd I'm told God hangs out with. The folks who don't have the extra baggage, the stuff we cling to, the personas and titles and self images that require so much attention, care and protection—much like you, Jonathan, when you called me two years ago.

Of course, the children must belong to this group. Like Mark Smalley, the poor kid you loved playing with at the creek, the kid with green teeth who couldn't hit a baseball and smelled funny. A nobody. It didn't matter. The friend you loved more than anyone. Maybe that's the way it is, Jonathan. Maybe when those things really don't matter, that's when we're the closest to God we ever get. Maybe that little boy with green teeth *was* Jesus.

These people live their lives unfiltered, more transparent, less calculating, less defended and so much more present, because they are not wrestling with looking good, having more, fearing embarrassment and impressing people. They are actually freer than most of us, less entangled in the smaller reality, more deeply connected to that rock-bottom Larger Reality that belongs to God.

Mothers, politicians, doctors, nice people, and professors struggle more than most; pastors and spiritual leaders most of all. They have so much to live up to, so much to protect and defend. These pillars in the community and the church invest so much emotional energy in protecting and defending their institutions, their doctrine or denomination, their memberships or special groups. They are masters at damage control and keeping up appearances.

The core problem is not that we're living inside a role or persona or reputation. We all do that because we all must do our jobs, wear different hats from time to time and fulfill our personal responsibilities. The problem is that we don't even know we're playing a role. We just go through life like this is all there is.

Many of us simply forget that we are more than the roles we have assumed. Deep down, we know better. We're not the degrees we've earned, the neighborhoods we live in, the famous people we know or the titles we wear. But we forget. And when we forget, everything goes to hell. It gets crazy.

The resulting delusions are like cockroaches: they can survive anything, even the crushing events that strip us of our falsehoods. We keep thinking that our carefully maintained image is who we actually are, or worse, that our pristine image is the person God loves.

When my image or reputation becomes threatened in any way, I instantly feel intimidated or diminished. I can feel the energy shift in my body, my muscles tighten and I become rigid and defensive, resistant to learning and changing. I usually either shut down and withdraw or go on the attack. I look for someone to be wrong. Those responses are the biggest clue that I've been living hard in the smaller reality. Feeling my own anxiety is often enough to jar my senses and pull me out of that defensive attitude.

Afterward, I can't even bash myself for falling into the same old pattern again. That's my false self getting hung up on being perfect—another trap. No one gets a lapel pin for "doing it right." In the Larger Reality, none of that crap matters. Honesty and personal awareness are all that's needed. Once I see it and I let the wider perspective in, I can feel the tension leave my heart and my body. I can feel His presence. And I'm more like JJ all over again.

The time has gotten away from me, Jonathan. I'm not forgetting about Gina and those developments. We need a whole day together just to walk and talk. Let's make it soon.

Lindsay and I love you, Jonathan.

S

Letter 20

September 10, 1989

Dear Jonathan,

Frankly, I am shocked. There are no words to describe what I feel. I can't wrap my mind around it. Are you telling me that your divorce is imminent? Thirty days, and it's done?

The only thing that makes any sense at the moment is recalling how much Gina always liked things neat and tidy. I can hear her voice in my head: "*I've* been faithful. *He* had the affair and destroyed our family. It's time to close this chapter of my life, wrap things up and move on. Jonathan broke the covenant. And that's that."

The prodigal husband has returned and the party could begin, but not if she has anything to say about it. It wouldn't be "right." Gina's not the one who screwed up. That was your deal. You don't "deserve" a welcome-home party, you "deserve" a kick to the curb with the rest of the trash.

Surely no one really thinks this way, Jonathan! Please tell me I'm absolutely wrong and completely off base.

But Gina couldn't go there. Relationships are too mysterious, complicated and fragile. A loyal soldier of Jesus, she wouldn't allow herself to fall or even to feel like she was falling. She must know at some level there will be a lot of sadness in accepting the fact that something she lived in failed so miserably. So she has chosen to remain inflexible and difficult. I'm so sorry about that.

I do think Gina still loves you, Jonathan. Deep down she still cares. But she loves being right even more. That's *her* affair partner—being right. What an unforgiving taskmaster, bound by this need to have the last word, to come out feeling on top. What a demanding, isolating and abusive "lover!"

My diagnosis sounds certain because I'm familiar with it all. I've been driven most of my life by that same deep insecurity. I can smell it a mile away. That's why no one is quicker than I am to judge her for such a brutal decision. I've made a hundred calls just like it, some just as destructive and life crushing. So my inner critic rises up saying, "What a hypocrite! You fool! Who are you to judge?" But I judge anyway. It's what we do when we feel completely out of control.

I can sense my own self-justifying, self-righteous thoughts spinning like crazy in my head right now—all in your defense, of course. But I can also see behind them. I see the insanity and inconsistencies behind my rash and damning judgments of Gina. And that helps; that does slow down the spinning.

From that wider perspective you and I have been talking about, I can see Gina as God may be seeing her. I can see you and myself too, all three of us as we really are: Desperate. Wounded. Fearful. Lost children. I think what I'm seeing for the first time ever is that the pouting and the pretentious—the *elder* brothers in all of our stories—are just as wounded and broken and needful of His grace as the returning and repentant prodigals. In fact, the ones who've done it right their whole lives may be in greater danger of forever missing the Father's love. Many do.

Jesus spent a lot of time grieving over His many failed attempts at liberating people from their "goodness." He must weep over all of us.

The Prodigal is the one who always misses the mark. Isn't that the definition of sin? I got that. People screw up. And they're easy to spot, people like you and me wandering from The Path, making God-awful choices again and again and again.

But those more aloof brothers and sisters, the ones who do everything right while tirelessly never missing the mark, usually spend their entire lives completely missing the point. They are *so right*, their energy and spirit often turn others away. Even worse, because they are *so right*, they remain blind to their own need for radical grace.

I have been a lifelong prodigal, fighting and cursing organized religion and its advocates. Even as a struggling follower of Jesus, I've proudly taken up what I thought was His cause and concern for the spiritual outcasts and moral reprobates. I've relished talking about His passion for the unlovable and unacceptable, while relentlessly castigating all the religious sons of bitches out there. I've been the champion of grace for every wandering, lost, face-in-the-mud prodigal, while cutting off and condemning my pious play-by-the-book brothers and sisters.

I've been judging the judgmental all my life. I seem to have missed the point as well.

Someday (please Lord, help me) I hope to have the heart of the Waiting Father who longs to embrace the faithful do-gooders as much as He loves those who stumble through the front door lost and dirty. Because He knows that in the ways that matter most, they are exactly the same. That will be a huge stretch for me—another miracle for sure.

Weren't we *all* invited to The Party?

The day will surely come when I must make amends with Gina and seek her forgiveness.

For now, I simply want to be with you, Jonathan. Let's take another long walk together down by the creek this weekend, before you move back to Nashville. It will probably be our last. Your father's house sold quickly. By the time you come back, the developers will have torn down your mother's home, dammed up the creek, and carved up those sixty acres into a hundred little lots. That land, as we have loved it, will be only a memory.

I know just the place for us to take that final stroll. It's where the creek makes a big turn in the middle of the pasture, just below the gravel road leading to the barn. It's the best spot on the creek. The water slows and pools up there, becoming deep enough to wade in up to our knees and look for frogs and lizards. Maybe see a snake.

Some of the best days in my life were spent there on that little beach, skipping rocks onto the opposite bank, launching sticks into the bumpy current as pretend battleships. Often I just sat in silence, watching the sun turn orange and disappear behind the pines while waiting for Lilly to call me for supper. It was an incredible time of peace and happiness and fun.

Maybe the comfort and sense of safety that surrounded me at the creek never left me because in the back of my mind, I knew that Lilly was not far away. So even when by myself, I somehow knew I was never alone. She would hear any cry for help because she was always listening for me. A comforting thought for any six-year old, and for a sixty-year old: to know and feel that someone cares about you that much.

I think you nailed it when you said all endings are not happy endings. That doesn't bring me much relief. I always had high expectations, hope that your situation would play out like a good movie and everyone would leave the theater feeling warm and satisfied and fulfilled. That didn't happen. I wish all the Christian books I've read were right and that God is always going to solve our problems. Isn't that why we pray, so that God can get on with mending and fixing the broken things in our lives, even the things that we broke?

The happy ending you longed for didn't happen. Gina will no longer be your wife. Strangely, I hear acceptance in your voice. I see it in your eyes. I feel it whenever I am with you. I also sense some joy tagging along. It leaves me in awe.

I'm not sure where to put all the sadness and grief, Jonathan, but I know it's all in there: the acceptance, the joy *and* the grief. What a strange concoction. How do we hold all of this? You seem to be doing just that. Holding it all. Embracing it all. And so it comes as no surprise to me that you are still teaching me, still inspiring me, probably more than ever. Just by being who you are. And that is something we have learned will always be enough.

Humor me while I attempt to trace this story of ours. It's like a three-act play filled with unexpected and unwelcome twists and turns.

Act I: Your successes, your determination and your drive. You dazzled me both on and off the field. We both know what happened.

Then came Act II: All the ways you encouraged me through your spiritual insights, the way you opened up the scripture, giving me that hunger to learn and grow. You delivered some sermons on God's grace and forgiveness that were life-changing for me.

I wasn't your best student. I complained and griped a lot. Challenged your ideas and gave the impression that I was above it all. But nothing you said, nothing you did was ever wasted on me.

I was pretty clueless back then. I had no idea how much I would some day be living out of that grace and drawing on the mercy you talked about. But it was always there, buried deep inside of me, waiting and wanting to rise up and give me hope.

That's why losing you was so hard for me. In spite of my resistance and hardness of heart, I knew you were a lifeline for me. You were my link to something real—to Lilly, to the past, and probably to God.

Then you called and Act III opened.

I wasn't expecting to learn this way from you, Jonathan. Not through your losses and suffering. Not through watching you fail and fall so far and suffer so much. Not through a day like today, watching you come to terms with Gina's decision to end your marriage.

I've never wanted to learn this way. I much prefer reading a good book or hearing a well-crafted sermon or playing one of those uplifting motivational tapes. I do want to learn, but I don't want to be taught. Not through hurting. Not through watching you suffer.

But, what must I be thinking? Of course I'm learning and growing this way. Actually, it's more like *un*-learning, letting go of my expectations and preconceived notions and hardened opinions of how life is supposed to work. Through this wild and mysterious un-learning, watching you walk through this dark and confusing time, I've discovered that suffering never was and never will be a malfunction of God's grace. It's just the way it is.

It cannot be taught. It can't be explained to anyone's satisfaction. We talk about it, experience it, and watch it play out in the lives of others. That's not an easy thing to do. Watching you suffer is pure agony for me.

And yet, wasn't this the way my own heart was finally primed and pried open for seeing God's goodness and mercy? Not by doing it right, but by doing it wrong again and again through my stupid choices and broken promises. God hides His mercy in those places we avoid the most and anticipate the least: our failures and our sins. He shrouds His grace and goodness in the places we dread the most: our powerlessness and our pain. I still don't like it. I still don't understand much of it. It's so counterintuitive, so contrary to my best thinking.

Nothing prepares us for this. We know we will experience setbacks and sorrow. But we're programmed to think of such suffering as a kind of interruption, a misstep, a momentary glitch, a religious hiccup—something we can handle or get around or get over quickly.

And none of it, we protest, should be necessary. It sounds like so much gloom and doom! Maybe I could read the Bible more, or be more loving to people, or think about becoming a missionary. Can we not avoid feeling hopeless and confused if we're just a little more careful, prayerful and wise in our choices? And when we do stumble, surely it's no big deal—just a short jog back to the sunny path of life.

Please stop smiling, Jonathan. I can see you shaking your head.

I know better. This hard grace is the way it is. God loves us too much to let us settle for our smaller realities where we believe everything can be neat and tidy and predictable.

It's like that quote your counselor, Jeremy, shared with you and Gina from Julian of Norwich:

"First there is the fall, and then the recovery. *Both* are the mercy of God."

There is no Plan B.

I had lunch yesterday with a good friend who's in Alcoholics Anonymous with me. For anonymity's sake, let me just call him Tom. When I met him eight years ago, I had no idea that he had a drinking problem.

I knew him and his wife through their son who played baseball for me at McCallie. Tom was the very popular senior minister at a large church outside of Chattanooga, and for one season he did all the devotionals with the team before our games.

After coming to a few AA meetings and getting over the shock of seeing me there, our friendship deepened and we started spending time together. A few weeks in, he asked me to be his sponsor.

He went six months without a drink—then got arrested on alcohol-related charges. His church board found out and they decided to step in.

He returned last week from four months of treatment in Arizona. Even though he went kicking and screaming, he came home saying it was the best thing he'd ever experienced. His stay out there may have salvaged his career. It definitely saved his life.

The downside is that he lost his position at the large church and was re-assigned to a smaller, rural church as an assistant. Professionally, it's a major step backwards. Personally, he's feeling very deflated and humiliated. The loss and shrinking of his authority and influence are killing him. He feels so much shame for letting down his friends, embarrassing his family and failing God miserably.

I won't bore you with the rest of the details, but I wanted to share this with you because of something he told me at lunch. "You know, Saul," he said, "this whole thing, all that we've been through, all the sadness and embarrassment? I'm thinking—well, it's sounds strange—but it's like we're on holy ground. It's the first time I've ever looked at things this way. You and I, a couple of drunks, walking on holy ground."

I wasn't sure what he meant by holy ground, so I just nodded and listened.

"I've been an ordained minister for twenty-seven years, a Christian even longer. I've never seen anything like this. I'm starting to get it, though. I think God has been up to something in my life for the longest time in order to bring me to this incredible place where I don't feel so bogged down with my role as a pastor, don't feel consumed with the idea of being a good Christian or living for God or feeling personally responsible for everyone's problems. All that pressure is gone. Today there's a focus on keeping things simple, staying out of the drama. There's not much for me to worry about now: stay sober, love my wife and kids. All that's left is this longing to be real. To be intimate with Jesus. To listen more. To love Him and let Him love me.

"Do you know what I'm talking about?"

"Yes, Tom," I said. "What you say reminds me a lot of the conversations I've had with my nephew." He kept going.

"This is the crazy part, Saul. I didn't learn any of this through my studies or from my prayer time. Things started coming together *after* my life fell apart. It sounds kind of simplistic, but could these things be showing up *because* I failed and fell so far that nothing I tried on my own could save me or bring me back? God, I'm so sad!—I cry now more than ever—but for some reason I feel more real and grounded and honest than ever. That's so weird. It's like I stumbled into this whole new world. It's not something I planned or would have ever chosen. But here I am anyway, sitting here with you. This is holy ground, isn't it, Saul?"

"Yes, Tom, I think it is. I never thought of it that way, but it's probably true. We are on holy ground. Maybe we've been here the whole time and just didn't know it."

We said our goodbyes and drove out of the parking lot. And I started thinking.

Maybe there's an Act IV for you and me, Jonathan, and this is the way it will open: The two of us are still walking together, yet now we know that all along we've been walking on holy ground. You and I moving along—guided, pushed, led and directed by some murky mixture of our own choices, but never without the strong and present underpinning of God's grace and mercy. He conceals these priceless gifts from us most of the time, then reveals them when we least expect it. That's *His* call. That's what makes it holy ground.

I'll see you Saturday at the creek.

Love,

L

Journal Entry 3

1992

Journal Entry 3

February 17, 1992

I believe in comebacks. When my life was falling apart, I *knew* there would be a comeback. But when it started, it was nothing like the one I had planned.

I believed that by embracing God's complete forgiveness and returning to the ministry, I would be transformed into a shining trophy of His undying love. Who could possibly understand God's unconditional acceptance better than I? I couldn't think of a more visible, more dramatic, or more convincing example of Christian renewal in action than me—newly chastened, insightful, and dedicated—resuming my pastoral duties before a duly impressed congregation.

But the people God assigned to me in that moment saw right through me, even though I considered myself a master at soothing ruffled feathers and deflecting people's anger and criticism. They knew that hidden behind my compliant demeanor was a restless heart, secretly creating an agenda that would bypass any effort on their part to put me on a path of humility and spiritual recovery.

I know now that the counsel I got that Monday morning was not textbook advice for every man who's had an affair. It was tailored specifically to me. I had been convinced that all I needed was the forgiveness of God and a heroic spiritual comeback.

They knew I needed more.

They demanded that I step back for a long season—work with my hands, get a job painting or landscaping—relying less on my charm and people skills. The purpose was for me to shrink my audience down to the One Person whose opinion really mattered. To lie low and hope for nothing but the truth. To live with my despair and guilt rather than medicate them with busyness and winning people's favor. To wait on His grace and tenderness alone to bring healing to my life. To slow down and focus for the first time ever.

God had a comeback planned all right. But His had a radically different shape, different timetable, different people, and very different methods from mine. And a completely different outcome.

I am grateful and awed by the tremendous healing I have experienced and the sheer miracle of surviving it all. But it has been so slow and confusing, filled with heartbreaks. The healing—the rebuilding of my life—has been a cumulative, tedious process, far from anything I could have anticipated. None of it has come from my doing any of those extraordinary, dramatic things I had planned, but from doing the most ordinary things every day. Hundreds of days and thousands of hours invested in being quiet, taking walks, doing mundane, un-heroic things:

Painful and tearful talks with Saul. Long conversations with my children, never easy, seldom pleasant. Endless counseling with Jeremy. Responding to gossip or misunderstandings with silence and a smile instead of explaining or defending myself. Giving myself permission, as Saul taught me, to simply be no one in particular.

Waiting in solitude. Writing in my journal. Learning about prayer in bits and pieces. Discovering fresh ways to read and listen to Scripture. Spending unrushed time with a handful of safe, caring men. Cutting the grass, washing my car. Surrendering my demands for quick fixes and instant validation. Finding joy in simple things. Acknowledging that my emotional repair and spiritual recovery are the most important things in my life. And that when I cry out for Him, He will hear me, and that will be enough.

This coming weekend I'll be moving into a $300-a-month apartment over a friend's garage. That's after being essentially homeless for two years. There was just no money. The divorce was not only emotionally devastating but a financial disaster on top of everything else.

For a while I maintained an unintended and ironic illusion of prosperity. A business associate leaving for seminary decided that the Mercedes he was driving gave people the wrong impression, so he invited me to take over the last year of his lease. And I spent those two homeless and broke years house-sitting a huge, gorgeous home near the Harpeth River.

The Mercedes and the mansion are gone now, replaced by the one-bedroom apartment and a twelve-year-old station wagon with a cracked back window and a side mirror held on with duct tape. My new business has been slow and time-consuming, but I am hopeful of turning things around, getting out of debt and repairing relationships with the kids. Modest and uncertain though it is, moving into my own apartment marks a new beginning.

In a sober moment at the end of his last call, Saul told me once again how much he loved me and how much I mean to him. That I was forever in his heart and, more important, forever in the grip of God and His grace. I've heard him say that to me a million times, and it feels as fresh and real as it did the first time. Maybe more so.

Just before hanging up, he also reminded me of an unforgettable line in a movie he loves. My precious uncle hasn't had a drop of alcohol in twenty years, but he's still an addict. Instead of vodka it's ESPN and his fascination with *The Natural*, the old baseball movie about an aging pitcher named Roy Hobbs, played by Robert Redford, who hopes for an incredible comeback. Sometimes I think Uncle Saul is convinced he is Roy Hobbs and will somehow, someday, hit the walk-off home run in the seventh game of the World Series.

That's when we laugh until we're crying. We've got to. We're both still crazy as hell and our brains play tricks on us all the time. But telling each other our wildest thoughts, our most demented fantasies, helps keep us sane. We're even willing to admit that there are times when we *still* want exactly what Redford's character says in the movie: That when we walk down the street, people would see us and they would say, "There goes Saul Bates," or "There goes Jonathan Goodson—*the best there ever was in this game*." We are nuts.

Glenn Close plays Iris, Roy's devoted girlfriend. In two short sentences she comforts a defeated and confused Hobbs by saying, "Well, I believe we have two lives. The life we learn with and the life we live with after that."

"That's you, Jonathan," Saul said. "Nothing has been wasted on you. Not a single day, not one defeat or death, not a single moment of despair. Every day His grace and His goodness have kept showing up in your life—holding you, comforting you, teaching you."

Saul loves reminding me that the last five years have not been about the amazing life experiences and heroic comeback of Jonathan Goodson. They've been about God's giving a man his heart back.

"Jonathan, I think you're ready," Saul said. "I think you're ready to live."

Saul, I think you're right.

Acknowledgments

Three people helped me write this book from start to finish. My friend Mark Somple told me out of the gate that if I simply spoke from my heart and put it on paper, something good would happen.

Brian Schrauger coached and encouraged me while I wrote the first and second drafts. Because of Brian, I actually wrote a book!

Then I asked John Perry to read my manuscript and offer up his experience and wisdom. He not only liked it, but he also got excited about it and joined me in the final edit—tightening and brightening the manuscript up to the day it was published.

Jadyn Stevens and Priscilla Stevens at Eveready Press were caring and careful editors of this project, and patient partners in creating the look and feel I wanted for the cover.

Many thanks to my colleagues and friends in the very special Juice Plus+® family who have been teaching and challenging and encouraging me for more than two decades to live with passion and pursue all of my dreams—including this book.

Then there's my real family, starting with my mother and father, Inez and Bevo Beavers, and my incredible brother, Curtis—my life-long heroes I think about every day and miss more than I ever imagined.

My nephew Curt Beavers and his mother, Jackie Beavers, have been the best mentors and partners I could ask for—supporting and loving me when I needed them the most.

I must express my love and gratitude for our six awesome children and their incredible spouses. Nathan, Stephanie, Lee Anne, Chip, Mary Jac, Mimi, Steve, Carter, Nikki, Emily and Dan—plus our large and ever expanding quiver of precious grandchildren.

Finally, there would have never been a book without Sally—my wife, partner, confidant, lover and cheerleader. Thank you for believing in me and helping me make this book a reality. I love you.

The Author

David Beavers was born in Atlanta in 1947, where he also attended Dykes High School. After receiving a degree in history from Vanderbilt in 1969, David joined the staff of Campus Crusade for Christ, working with college students throughout the Southeast. He then attended Dallas Theological Seminary where he earned a Th.M. (Master of Theology) in 1977. He served in churches in Nashville, Tennessee and Clearwater, Florida, and directed a counseling and teaching ministry known as **The Word on Your Family**, based in Nashville.

In 1988, David launched his career with National Safety Associates (NSA, Memphis, Tennessee), the maker of Juice Plus+®. David is currently a National Marketing Director with NSA and works out of his home in Nashville.

David and his wife, Sally, were married in 1996. Together they have six grown children and fifteen grandchildren. Sally taught the third grade at Oak Hill School for seventeen years, before retiring in 2002.

David is a teacher at heart, and loves coaching and mentoring people in their personal development. This is his first novel.

Additional copies of *Letters to Jonathan*
may be purchased at Amazon.com
or by contacting the author.

David Beavers
306 Page Road
Nashville, TN 37205

david@thebeavers.net

615-364-2737

www.davidbeavers.net

www.letterstojonathan.com